Moon Over Montana

Other Books by Caroline Fyffe

McCutcheon Family Series

Montana Dawn
Texas Twilight
Mail-Order Brides of the West: Evie
Mail-Order Brides of the West: Heather
Moon Over Montana
Mail-Order Brides of the West: Kathryn
Montana Snowfall
Texas Lonesome
Montana Courage

~~~*~~~

Prairie Hearts Series

Where the Wind Blows
Before the Larkspur Blooms
West Winds of Wyoming
Under a Falling Star
Whispers on the Wind
Where Wind Meets Wave

~~~*~~~

Stand Alone Western Historical

Sourdough Creek

Stand Alone Contemporary Women's Fiction

Three And A Half Minutes

Moon Over Montana

Montana

A McCutcheon Family Novel

Book Five

Caroline Fyffe

Edited by Caitlin Alexander
Copy edited by Pam Berehulke
Beta Reader Kandice Hutton
Cover design by Kelli Ann Morgan
Interior book design by Bob Houston eBook Formatting

Proudly Published in the United States of America

ISBN #978-0-9897025-7-7

*Dedicated to my dear
mother-in-law,
Patricia Fyffe, with love*

Prologue

Silver Fish, Montana Territory, Early June 1886

Fox Dancing lifted the leather flap of the tepee and let her eyes adjust to the inky blackness of the night. Dark thunderheads blanketed the sky in every direction, covering the moon's glow and promising a hellish storm within the hour.

The night I've been waiting for. One that will erase any tracks I might leave behind.

The camp was quiet. She waited patiently, her knapsack packed at her side, and beside it, her bow and quiver. She fingered the small leather pouch that dangled from a cord around her neck, and pushed from her mind the crouching cougar of fear that threatened to weaken her heart. The amulet held her talisman, formed of several downy tufts from the underbelly of a baby eagle, mixed with the tail feather from its mother.

Because a vision quest was required only of the young braves, she'd had to sneak off last year against the protests of her father's two wives. Her mothers' worried glances had fueled her determination all the more. The moment she'd seen the eagle's nest perched high in a craggy cliff off the mountainside, understanding had flooded her heart. The Great Spirit had put it there just for her. After climbing the sheer wall, she'd wrestled the feisty chick to get a fistful of its down. She wore her talisman now as she always did. It would protect her throughout the journey.

Her grandfather, Talking Tree, was the only one who understood her. She could no more stay in the tepee mending and cooking with the other girls than fly like an eagle. After months of begging, he'd taught her to ride when she was only four, to hunt and track the year after that. And she was a good hunter! Unafraid of the kill. By the time she turned sixteen years last month, the others were frightened of her and gave her a wide berth.

Everyone except Painted Bear Stone. Whereas the other young warriors thought her strange, her strength and wit seemed to charm Painted Bear Stone. Three years older, he'd made it a habit to watch over her since she was a young girl, even when she'd asked him not to. He teased her unmercifully, forcing her to dig her nails into her palms until they bled. It was as if he lived to make her life miserable. His playful smile and sharp gaze knew her every move even before she did, and haunted her dreams. But this year, his attention had changed. Turned into something else, much to her dismay. To her utter shock, he had asked her father for her five nights ago.

She would be his wife by the next moon.

At least, that is what the village thinks. They believe once I marry I will forget my desire to ride and hunt, to protect my people. They think I should settle into a woman's way. Gathering food, cooking meals, mending clothes—and having babies. A shudder ran through her body. *Instead, I will go to my white half brother, the one I've heard our father speak about.*

The idea had come in a dream. Her father's whispered conversations about the great son he had sired, the one who lived in the white world, sated her unconscious like raindrops in spring until she knew what she must do. She would miss her family here, but at least she wouldn't be shackled to a husband—or be forced to move to the reservation, where she would die without the wind in her hair, a horse galloping under her, and the freedom to come and go at will.

In the dark of the tepee, she remained motionless. One false move now could jeopardize her plan. She needed to be smart, like her grandfather had taught her to be. At the thought of his ailing health, her heart seized. Annoyed by her weakness, she pushed her emotions away.

A soft whistle reached her ears. She took one last look at Biting Horse and Crow Foot Woman, each deep asleep inside a heavy buffalo robe. This would be the last time on this earth that she would see them. She'd been lucky. Wakhan Thanka had blessed her with amicable mothers. She would miss them.

When the signal came a second time, Fox Dancing whispered a silent prayer of deliverance, then picked up her things. *I am a fierce warrior. Nothing can stop me.* The words played over and over in her mind as she crept silently out into the night toward the horse pasture where her mare would be ready and waiting.

Chapter One

Y Knot, Montana Territory, July 1886

"**M**other!" Charity McCutcheon scrambled from the stagecoach and rushed into her mother's embrace. Oh, how she'd longed to feel these arms so many times while living far from home in Texas. The familiar scent of sweet lemony butter soothed Charity's heart. "How did you know we'd be arriving today?"

Her father and the rest of the family waited on the boardwalk in front of the Y Knot stage office. "A very special birdie told us," Claire replied, still holding her close. "And we're all indebted. We wouldn't have missed your homecoming for anything."

Charity slid a conspiratorial glance toward Brandon. The happy crinkle around his eyes and the squeeze of his warm hand around her own gave her his answer.

"You didn't think I'd let an occasion like this go by, did you, darlin'?" he asked, one side of his mouth lifting in a half smile. "Everyone's eager to see you home safe and sound."

With his hat pushed up, she had a perfect view of his face. She almost lost her ability to breathe, he looked so handsome.

Her worries that he might have second thoughts suddenly seemed just plain silly.

"I don't know if I should hug you or beat your bottom red, missy," her father boomed. Flood McCutcheon gathered her into his arms as the others shook Brandon's hand or kissed his cheek. "You scared the life right out of us when we received Brandon's telegram. Sneaking off to Texas without a by-your-leave! You should be ashamed of yourself. A McCutcheon is always straightforward and honest."

Cocooned in her father's embrace, she felt like a child again, with a scraped knee or bee-stung finger. His words were harsh, but only because he loved her so much. Happiness surged in her chest as she thanked the Lord above for such a loving family.

"I'm so glad you're home, princess," he whispered. "In all honesty, the place has been too quiet without you to mix things up. We need a little of your spark."

She heard him sniff and wondered if he was also battling tears.

The stage rolled away after the last passenger disembarked, leaving their luggage stacked on the boardwalk, and Brandon's and Charity's horses transferred from their spot tied to the back of the stage to the hitching rail.

As soon as their pa let her go, Luke pulled Charity close. "Who're you kiddin', Pa? You've never whipped Charity once in her life. Not like us boys. It's your leniency that's created the problem in the first place." He hugged her tight, causing her unshed tears to fall. "She's spoiled to the core."

Impatient, Faith dragged Charity from Luke's arms. "A girl *should* have a mind of her own," she said, then took her turn to hug her sister-in-law. "Keeps the men in her life on their toes."

Brandon groaned loudly, while Mark and Matt, Charity's older brothers, nodded emphatically. "And don't we know it," Brandon said. "Did you know Charity was a schoolteacher in Texas?" Everyone gasped. "We have stories that'll take a month to tell."

"It's so good to have you back, dear girl," Faith murmured. "I've missed you more than you could know." They stepped apart. Amy and Rachel followed with hugs, both women's growing pregnancies evident. Then came Matt and Mark.

Charity looked around. "Where're all the children? Billy and Adam, Colton, Dawn, Beth, and Cinder. My goodness. And also little Holly. I'll bet she's growing like a weed."

"Back at the ranch with Esperanza and her grown niece." Faith sent Luke a flirtatious glance. "Dinner out at Cattlemen's doesn't come around often, so we're all making a night out of it by leaving the children at home. Lucky's back at the ranch helping with the young'uns."

"Besides," Mark added. "We want to be able to hear what you have to share about our little brother, John, and his new wife, Lily. That's a mite difficult with all the babies and toddlers we have."

Charity couldn't help a little hop of excitement. "Oh, Mother. Lily is *so* lovely. You're going to adore her. She's from Germany and has beautiful long blond hair. But that's not what makes her so special; it's her goodness and…" She took in the faces of her family, each so dear to her, as they listened intently. "She and John are so in love. It's a wonderful thing."

She glanced at the buildings along Main Street. To an outsider this rugged cow town with its clapboard structures and dirt streets would seem ordinary, but to her it was anything but, and it held a special place in her heart. Y Knot seemed the same, yet different too—perhaps her perception was what had changed the most.

She stepped closer to Brandon and found his hand. Their fingers entwined. By the looks she was receiving, everyone seemed to know what must be coming. She and Brandon hadn't moved a foot from each other's side since exiting the stagecoach. It felt good to finally know where her destiny rested. Still, the thought of their marriage announcement tonight sent a flock of butterflies racing around inside.

"You should see Texas," she said to take her mind off her unsettled feelings. She let go his hand and stretched her arms wide. "It's big and desolate and dry." Not all the time, though, she thought, remembering the rainstorm the day her Texas cousin Chaim took the bullet that almost killed him. "I didn't realize just how blue our skies are here in Montana until I left them behind."

"And vast," Brandon added.

She nodded. So many things here at home she'd taken for granted, but she wouldn't anymore. "Uncle Winston and Aunt Winnie are *such* good people. I felt as if I'd known them forever, and loved them right from the start. The ranch is beautiful, so different from ours and yet the same." Everyone nodded, her meaning clear. "And our cousins are fine people too. At first I wasn't sure about Dustin, but he turned out nice in the end. He and John almost came to blows over Lily." She laughed at the surprised looks. "Actually they *did* on John and Lily's wedding night. Brandon not only showed up to save me from a rattlesnake, but had the funds to bail John and Dustin out of jail—"

"Whoa, now, sweetheart," Brandon said with a chuckle. "Save some for later."

"I will. I will. I just think the whole family needs to take a trip to Texas so they'll experience firsthand what I'm talking about."

"Hold up, Charity, you just got home," Flood said. His brown vest hugged his chest; he was as tall and fit as her brothers. "We'll take one day at a time. No more fancy trips without telling us—or, I should say, without us." His face was set, but she knew that with a kiss to his cheek she could persuade him to say yes to just about anything.

Excitement and longing zipped through Charity. She missed her relatives and friends in Rio Wells already, a consequence of her travels and expanding her circle of loved ones.

Her father gave her a stern eye. "We'll all make it to Texas—someday. To visit John and his new bride. But for right now, I hope you and Brandon are hungry." He slung his arm around Brandon's shoulder and pulled him close, like he did often with her brothers.

A touched expression lit Brandon's face and Charity had to look away or cry. This was going to be so good for Brandon, for them. Now that the decision had been made, she couldn't wait to become his wife.

"We have the large round table reserved at Cattlemen's," her pa went on. "I say we head that way now before Jackson or Lenore think we've changed our minds and give it to someone else. You can regale us with every single thing that happened while we get some grub into our bellies."

"I second that," Luke said.

Everyone nodded. When they turned, Charity threaded her arm through her mother's, just like she used to as a girl. Their energetic talk and laughter garnered more than a few curious glances. Some acquaintances waved and called out to

Brandon or Charity. A man dressed in a raggedy top hat and vest came riding down the street on a mule, a tear-shaped instrument in his hands. He smiled and strummed a few chords as he passed.

"Who's that?" Charity asked.

"Y Knot's own town minstrel," her mother said. "Casper Slack. You never know where he'll show up next—to sing you a song. It's really quite nice."

As they neared the hotel, Charity navigated a step on the boardwalk, glancing away from Luke's reenactment of Colton trying to saddle his new horse. Her gaze slid past a man standing in front of the leather shop, and she stopped abruptly when she recognized him. Her heart gave a happy leap. "Chance!"

Smiling from ear to ear, Chance Holcomb and a young woman with a head of curly blond hair started their way.

"Miss Charity, it's darn fine to see you. I've heard all the news about your time in Texas and John getting married from the telegrams Brandon has sent back." He laughed and shook his head. "It's still hard to believe since I haven't seen John since he went away to school. Why all the hands at the Heart of—"

He stopped abruptly and turned to the woman on his arm. "Forgive me, I've forgotten my manners. Charity, this is my wife, Evie Holcomb." The proud ring to his tone was unmistakable. "Evie, this is Charity McCutcheon"—he motioned with his head—"the boys' little sister. She's been away for three months. That's Brandon Crawford, her, uh—the sheriff of Y Knot."

Brandon smiled and touched the brim of his hat.

"Wife!" Charity blurted, taking in the pretty woman in the lovely yellow dress. Her features were delicate and she had blue eyes full of wonder. Where the heck had Chance found her?

"I'm pleased to make your acquaintance, Miss McCutcheon." Evie's hand, tucked into the crook of Chance's elbow, flexed.

Embarrassed over her outburst and the hurt in Evie's eyes, Charity hurried to say, "I'm sorry. That was rude. I'm so very glad to meet you too, Mrs. Holcomb, but I do have to say I am a bit shocked. It must have happened very quickly."

She sent Chance an apologetic glance for her blunder.

"We all think Chance is a sweetheart," Charity went on, "which I'm sure you're well aware of, because you married him." She couldn't stop the wide smile from taking over her face. "I'm certainly happy to have another woman in town. Do you ride?"

"Not well. Chance is teaching me, though."

"You should see their home," Faith said, holding on to Luke's arm. "It's beautiful. And Evie's stove is the most extravagant contraption any of us have ever seen. Amy and I both want one just like it."

"That's so true, Charity." Amy fairly glowed with excitement. "It practically fills the whole kitchen. Evie's planning a baking day with all of us. Now that you're home, you can come along." Her shy sister-in-law looked lovely today, and adoration radiated between her and Mark.

"A house? When I left that was just an open piece of land with a barn and some fancy French cattle. You sure have been busy."

One of her brothers cleared his throat. Then a chuckle eased its way around the group.

Charity glanced back. "What?"

"He's been busy, all right." Luke's eyebrow peaked.

Chance's face resembled the red saddle blanket on her horse.

"Oh!" Charity couldn't help herself. She stepped forward and gave Evie a hug, then cuffed Chance on the arm. "I think that's wonderful. Congratulations." Heat wove around inside her belly when she thought of her and Brandon making a baby. Maybe by this time next year her arms would be full.

"Come on, folks," Flood said. "We haven't made much progress to the restaurant. Chance, we're headed to Cattlemen's for an early supper. We'd be pleased if you and Evie would join us. You're practically family. It's our treat."

Chance looked down into Evie's eyes.

"I insist," Claire said, before they had an opportunity to say no. "I haven't seen you for a month of Sundays, Chance. And I'm sure Evie would enjoy some time with other women. My gosh, for days on end it's just you and the cattle."

"Well, when you put it like that," Chance said, chuckling, "how can I refuse? But I'm paying for Evie and me."

"You'll do no such thing." Claire gave him a stern look. "We've meant to invite the two of you out to the ranch since your marriage. This will make up for our bad manners."

Charity smiled. "Good. I'm glad that's settled."

She and Brandon led the way to the hotel. Before they went in, Brandon pulled her to the side, letting the rest pass. "I'm going to poke my head in the office for one minute and speak with Jack if he's there. It won't take long." His gaze slid to the sheriff's office next door and his expression went hard.

"Promise you'll be quick?"

"Of course. We have big things to talk about." He leaned in close. "I wish I could kiss you."

"I know. Me too."

"And we can't make the announcement until I speak with Flood. It wouldn't be proper."

Charity couldn't stop this odd feeling that something was going to go wrong. Somehow, some way, their intentions would be jumbled. Just like all the other things that had kept them apart through the years.

"You'll speak with him today, at the party, right?"

He gave her a smile that had the power to send her stomach somersaulting. Since the hayloft in Rio Wells, her awareness of Brandon had changed. Grown deeper. She'd experienced a sliver of what husbands and wives held special. The secret power that connected them. She couldn't wait to be man and wife.

"That's our plan. Now go inside and get comfortable," he said. "I'll be right in. I'll take Flood aside and do the asking. You don't think he'll say no, do you?"

"Charity and Brandon, are you going to stand out there all night?"

Her mother had come outside looking for them. The light shining in her eyes said she knew exactly what they were discussing.

"We'll be right there," Charity called. She gave her mother a smile and turned back to Brandon. "Say hello to Jack for me."

At the mention of his deputy, Brandon gave an exasperated sigh. "He's the only one I'm not anxious to see."

Chapter Two

Brandon covered the ground between the hotel and the sheriff's office. It was good to be back in Y Knot. He hadn't realized how much he'd missed the place. He paused, taking a good look down the street. A few horses dozed in the sun in front of the Hitching Post Saloon. Farther down at Lou and Dritt's boardinghouse, someone swept the boardwalk in front, pushing the dirt into the street. He grinned. In one day the dust would settle right back onto the wood. Glancing across to Lichtenstein's Provisions, he wondered how the feisty German fared, as well as his timeworn clerk, Mr. Simpson. That old codger hadn't missed a day since Brandon had taken over as sheriff.

These were his people. He'd been looking out for their welfare for a good number of years. They were his friends, and the only family he knew. And of course, there were the McCutcheons. They'd be true family once he and Charity tied the knot. He swallowed down a small lump of emotion. A vision of Charity maturing over the years brought a smile to his lips.

Charity. *My girl.* She'd finally said yes.

The door of Berta May's sewing shop opened and Berta May stepped out. Her smile transformed her face into a glow of happiness. "I thought that was you, Sheriff Crawford! Welcome back. Seems like you've been gone forever. How long has it been?"

"Over two months."

"Everyone is sure going to be glad to see you back. I know I am." She drew out the word *I*, and then smiled shyly. "Let me know if there's anything you need. Anything at all."

He couldn't miss when the handsome, aging seamstress batted her lashes at him, and he smiled. "Thank you, Berta May. It's darn good to be home. If I think of anything, I'll let you know."

"You do that, Sheriff. Still, I'm baking you a pie tomorrow. Yes, sir, that's exactly what I'm going to do. I hope you like apple—Brandon."

He nodded. "My favorite."

"That settles it. Look for it bright and early."

Stepping across the threshold of his office, Brandon stopped short. The disarray hit him like a board in the face. Jack Jones sat behind Brandon's desk, asleep. The deputy's muddy boots were propped up over a mountain of papers, and his hat covered his face. A long, rippling snore almost woke him, but not quite.

Brandon stepped over and knocked Jack's boots off the desk. When the deputy's feet hit the floor, his head jerked with an angry growl. He blinked several times, as if he thought Brandon was a mirage.

Brandon's smile was tight. "What? You thought I wasn't coming back? That I was leaving the good citizens of Y Knot in your care forever?"

"Brandon! When did you arrive?" Jack stood, smacking his lips as he pushed his scraggly hair out of his eyes.

Brandon looked around. "Where's Craig?"

"Quit the week after you left."

Anger twisted up Brandon's spine, but he took hold of his temper. "And you didn't see fit to let me know?"

"I couldn't. The telegraph line in Rio Wells was down. You said that yourself when you telegrammed from San Antonio."

"A week after I left Y Knot, I sent you three telegrams from Denver—before I left Colorado for Texas."

Jack had the decency to look ashamed. "Guess it slipped my mind."

"More like you enjoyed your unchallenged authority around here. Did you run Craig off?" Brandon went over to the wall where the wanted posters hung. It only took a second to see that a couple were outdated; he recognized the faces of criminals already arrested or killed. He looked over his shoulder. "Where are the new flyers?"

Jack tipped his head toward a chair behind the door. "Over there. I'm switching 'em out later today."

Resigned, Brandon nodded. "Well, why don't you get to it while I go through this mess on my desk." He pushed some papers aside with his finger and sat. "Anything important happen in my absence?"

Jack pulled the pins from the corners of a poster. "I helped solve a crime that almost killed old man Klinkner."

Brandon looked up from his chair. "Oh?"

"Yeah, his steam engine blew up and his leg got broke. Lucky he and Hayden weren't killed. At first, everyone thought it was an accident, but after snooping around, me and the sheriff in Pine Grove discovered different. Turned out Abner Lundgren's wife didn't like losing business to the Klinkner mill in Y Knot."

Brandon nodded and stood. He needed to get back to the restaurant. Ten minutes had already passed and Charity would come looking for him any moment. Ever since she'd agreed to marry him, things had been going along well. He didn't want to start this new chapter off on the wrong foot. "That was good work, Jack. I appreciate you taking the reins while I was gone."

"You're not mad at me?"

"I'm plenty perturbed."

Jack cast his gaze to the floor, where a light coat of dust crunched under Brandon's boots. "I'll get this place cleaned up right away."

Brandon took a step toward the door. "I'll be over at Cattlemen's having supper." He'd crossed the threshold when Jack called him back.

"I almost forgot. You got some important-looking mail while you were away."

By the battered envelope Jack handed him, it seemed his deputy had been curious as to the contents.

"Thanks," Brandon said, taking the post.

"I couldn't help but notice it's from a US marshal in Kansas City."

Brandon stared at the logo stamped on the front. "So it is." His nonchalance was difficult to keep up.

The job. Months had passed since he'd sent the letter. When he hadn't heard anything, he figured James Timberlake had forgotten who Brandon Crawford was. Deputy to a US federal marshal, especially one as famous as Timberlake, would be a huge step up in his career.

But one that would take him away from Y Knot. Would Charity go with him? The ranch was everything to her and all she ever talked about.

He'd known things with Charity were too good to be true. They should have gotten married in San Antonio, the same night as John and Lily. Then she'd have to go with him. Torn, he stepped outside and gazed up into the sky, not knowing what to think. He didn't want to miss this opportunity, but he didn't want to lose the love of his life either. Seemed hard choices had come home to roost.

Wait a minute. I haven't gotten the job yet. Maybe Timberlake's turning me down. There had to be more than a few men interested in such a good position.

Disappointment registered at the possibility. He'd dreamed of a federal career since the day the silver star of Y Knot had been pinned to his vest. Why he felt so strongly about it, he wasn't quite sure—except that it had been a federal marshal who had avenged his parents' murder.

With a sigh, he started for Cattlemen's.

When he was halfway to the restaurant, Charity opened the door and hurried out to meet him. He folded the envelope and stuffed it in his back pocket.

"I thought you said you'd only be gone a moment," she said, laughter in her voice. "I can see I'm going to have some stiff competition for your affections now that we're back in Y Knot." He'd closed the remaining space between them. "I won't be jealous, though, I promise. I know there's enough of you to go around."

Charity's strawberry-blond hair flowed around her shoulders. Even after days in a stagecoach, she was still the most gorgeous woman he'd ever set eyes on.

She cocked her head as she looked up at him. "Is everything all right? You seem funny."

He wasn't ready to tell her. Not yet. She'd been so happy during their travels home. And now today. It wasn't right to burst her bubble before she had a full chance to enjoy it.

Brandon patted his stomach. "I think I'm just hungry. I haven't had a good meal in days."

She looped her arm through his and hugged it to her. They went together into the hotel. "You're not getting a good steak yet, cowboy. You still have some important business with my father to take care of. You haven't changed your mind, have you?"

He hadn't, but had fate changed it for him?

Chapter Three

Charity all but floated across the dining room floor. With Brandon at her back and the gaze of her whole family on her, she glided into the seat next to her mother. Brandon helped push her in, then settled next to her.

Lenore Saffelberg came forward, pad and pencil in hand. "Ready to order?" she asked, looking at Claire McCutcheon.

Charity reached under the table and found Brandon's hand. If she didn't know different, he almost looked scared to death. But that wasn't possible. Brandon didn't fear anything. She'd learned that firsthand in Texas. He enfolded her hand in both of his and gave it a warm, comforting squeeze. When she cut her gaze over to her father, she found him smiling at them with pride.

"Patience, sweetheart," Brandon whispered. "Just as soon as Flood orders his dinner, I'll speak with him."

When Lenore finished with Claire's order, she came to Charity. "Welcome home," she said. A twinkle in the waitress's eye made her look pretty. "What would you like for supper?"

"Thanks, Lenore. Since this *is* a celebration, I think I'll have a filet. Petite cut, please. Not quite on-the-hoof red—but pretty close. Just make sure it's not dead broke. Broke is okay—green broke too."

Her brothers chuckled at her old girlhood shenanigans. She glanced across the table and winked, waiting to hear the soft *tsk-tsk* she expected from her mother any second. She wasn't disappointed.

Lenore's eyebrow arched as she wrote on her pad. "Very well." A curious smile curled her thin lips. "Mashed potatoes or rice?"

Charity liked Lenore. Even though she teased her sometimes, she knew the sentiment was mutual. The twenty-six-year-old spinster kept to herself and rented one of the small rooms behind the hotel. Her life was somewhat of a mystery, except that she'd come into town alone and was rarely seen anywhere but right here in this dining room. Tonight, her soft-looking mousy brown hair was braided with a yellow ribbon that matched her apron and twisted into a bun at the nape of her neck. She had a sharp tongue at times, but that was mostly with the men.

"Rice, please."

Lenore moved on to Evie Holcomb. With everyone's attention shifted to Chance's new wife, Charity took the opportunity to glance at Brandon. Oh, how she loved this man. With his hat off—a rare occasion—she admired his wavy dark hair, thick and trimmed around his ears. Now she knew why he'd ducked into the barbershop in Denver when the stage stopped. The plans for this welcome-home party must have already been put into motion before then. His return gaze caressed her face, making her insides tingle. As his wife, she'd get to spend hours alone with him. The thought was heady. Imagine that. Day and night in his arms and it would all be perfectly respectable.

Feeling her face heat at her naughty thoughts, she almost giggled. Now she understood her sisters-in-law's excitement when her brothers were scheduled to return home. They'd spend hours on their appearance, changing their dresses so many times it seemed foolish. Charity used to think they'd lost their souls to her brothers. Now it made perfect sense that what they anticipated was freely given and cherished.

Brandon gave Charity a nod and pushed his chair back. Lost in her own little world, she was surprised to find Lenore had finished and now walked quickly toward the kitchen. Brandon circled the table and whispered into her father's ear. Flood's gaze met hers for one split instant, then he nodded and followed Brandon into the hotel lobby.

Charity could hardly breathe. She reached for her water but drew her hand back quickly, as its tremor would surely slosh water onto the tablecloth and everyone would want to know why. She'd best wait until Brandon and her father returned. When Jackson came up to the table with a bottle of wine and a white cloth draped over his arm, she let go a calming breath. The manager's brow crinkled, looking around for Flood.

"I'll try the wine," Matthew McCutcheon said. As the oldest brother, Matt filled in whenever their father wasn't around. "Pa had some important business he needed to attend to."

Mark chuckled, and Amy and Faith exchanged expectant smiles. "He'll be back in a few minutes, I'm sure."

"Very well," Jackson said. The dining room host made a show of presenting the bottle to Matt. After her brother nodded, Jackson set about with the corkscrew. He poured a small amount of wine into Matthew's glass and waited while her brother tasted it.

"This will do very well, Jackson. And I'm sure we'll need another bottle. This one will barely give us all a taste."

"Yes, sir." The short man went around the table to the women first. After he'd finished pouring Charity's glass, her mother leaned in close.

"You look beautiful, sweetheart. The Texas air agreed with you."

The compliment soothed away some of Charity's nerves. "Rio Wells was nice while I was there, Mother, but I can't tell you how much I missed Montana. There's nothing like our high mountain air—it's so clean and fresh. I found myself longing for it more times than I can count." *Especially when the hot-spring gases drifted over, making the whole town of Rio Wells smell like rotten eggs.*

Claire's smile was understanding. "I so agree with you. But was it just the Montana air that you missed? If you say yes, I'll be sad."

"Of course not! I missed my family and friends the most—from the bottom of my heart. Y Knot is all I'll ever need. I never want to leave again, unless it's just for a visit. And look what happened while I was gone. Chance has up and found a wife. I'm still amazed." Chance and Evie were in discussion with Luke and Faith. Charity was certain she and her mother wouldn't be overheard. "Evie is beautiful. It's hard for me to picture them together, him being such a shy bachelor when I left."

Her mother nodded. "Evie was a mail-order bride. She came all the way from St. Louis."

Distracted, Charity didn't immediately pick up on what her mother had just said. *How many words does it take to make a man's intentions known and then ask permission to get married?* She glanced at the lobby entrance in hopes she'd see her father and Brandon returning. Tapestry drapes, carpet, and the shimmering lanterns were her only view.

The comment about Evie finally sank in. "Mail-order bride! I remember seeing the advertisement in the paper sometime in the spring. Well, I'll be. Chance is braver than I thought."

"I'd say Evie is the brave one. To leave everything familiar to venture west and marry a man she didn't know." Claire shook her head. "That thought is quite amazing. Brave for Chance too, I guess. But not quite the same. With a man outweighing a woman by twice as much sometimes, one has to trust completely."

Charity didn't quite understand her mother's point, but she noticed a slight shadow cross her usually bright eyes. Before she had time to wonder overly long on the matter, her mother smiled. "Look at Chance now. I guess loneliness will do that to a fellow—make him take up the pen and write to a bride agency." Her mother laughed quietly and patted her hand. "Love is a beautiful thing, sweetheart. And I have more to tell about Hayden Klinkner. We'll save that for girl talk tonight."

Shock registered in Charity. "Hayden!" That flirt had promised he'd never settle down. Before she could say any more, Brandon and her father returned from the lobby.

Charity held her breath as they took their seats. She reached over and clutched Brandon's hand. From the corner of her eye, she saw him swallow.

Flood took his wineglass and stood, holding the goblet high. "I'd like to propose a toast to Brandon and Charity's return. Y Knot was much too quiet without them. Welcome home."

Everyone looked at him expectantly, surely thinking he was going to say something else. A moment of fear sliced through Charity's heart. *Welcome home?* She gripped Brandon's hand but couldn't make herself look at his face.

Murmuring filled the silence as the group picked up their glasses, again welcoming the two home. Charity could hardly stand the suspense. Was her father torturing her on purpose? Had Brandon changed his mind at the last moment and chickened out? Her sisters-in-law gazed at her now, as did Evie and her mother.

"*And*," her father went on in his booming voice.

At the word, everyone let out a collective sigh of relief and some even laughed. They sat straight in their chairs, waiting for Flood's announcement.

"I'm so proud to offer my congratulations to my beautiful daughter, Charity, and my soon-to-be son, Brandon, on their upcoming nuptials. I couldn't be happier about it if it were my own wedding to be planned." He glanced at his wife and winked. "May they be as happy as Claire and I have been for all these years!" Flood waved his arm until Jackson came running. "We'll need a couple bottles of your best champagne."

A roar of approval resounded around the table. Charity felt her smile grow wider as a joy she'd never experienced before lifted her heart. Claire got up and pulled Charity to her feet and hugged her. Next, she hurried over to Brandon and did the same.

Finally! Charity and her knight in shining armor had overcome their obstacles and would soon be man and wife. It was right, and felt oh so good.

Luke circled the table to shake Brandon's hand. "It's about time, Crawford. I've had my money on you for years, but recently started to wonder. Just like Pa, this news is the best I've heard all year. When's the big day?"

When Charity looked at Brandon to see what he would say, she was taken aback. His expression was hard as he struggled to smile. *What's going on?*

"As far as I'm concerned"—she pulled away from Faith and Amy and wiggled close to Brandon—"tonight after supper. We've waited long enough and planned all the way from Texas. This is what we want."

Her mother, who'd followed her, stiffened. "Not on your life, missy," Claire said. "I've only one daughter and I've been patiently waiting, probably longer than you have, for this announcement. I want a little time to plan and prepare. One more month won't kill you and will make me immensely happy."

"But, Mother, we were counting on right away." She hugged Brandon's arm tightly. "Shouldn't it be up to us if we don't want a big, fancy wedding? Just a few words with Reverend Crittlestick and all of you as witnesses. Here, tonight. Simple. That is, if the preacher is in town."

"Hold on, sweetheart. Your mother has a good point. One month is hardly anything." Brandon put on a good show of smiling, but something behind his eyes scared her to death.

Shocked, she gaped at him. He calmly took a drink of his wine, and settled his glass back on the white tablecloth. She and Brandon had discussed this at length on their way home. Both knew there'd be some resistance from her parents, but he'd promised her they wouldn't let anyone talk them into waiting. Acknowledging their on-again, off-again history, the best way to make sure the wedding happened was to do it immediately upon their return.

Brandon put his arm around her and gave a squeeze. "Well, Charity, what do you think? Should we give your mother a month as a thank-you for putting up with all our shenanigans over the years?"

What *was* that she saw in the back of his eyes? "We talked this point to death on the stage, Brandon. I can't believe you're agreeing." A bubble of hurt constricted her heart. He was siding with her father and mother already. Maybe that was to be expected. Maybe he felt pressure as the new son-in-law to go along, keep the peace—win their love. He didn't need to do that. But his searching, whiskey-colored eyes beseeched her, and her resolve crumbled. She was powerless against that expression.

Regret at the thought of waiting outweighed her puzzlement over Brandon's strange mood. She couldn't figure him out, but she'd worry about that later. For now, she'd make the best of the situation. Her family had done so much for her; this was the least she could do for them.

She turned and took her mother's hands in her own. "I think that's a fine idea. I can just imagine all the tea parties we'll have going over the details. Fine, one month from today. That will give us time to do everything we need. But not a day more."

"And we'll have a party out at our place this Saturday night," Luke said. "To announce it. Faith and I have had a shindig planned for weeks, to christen our new barn. We'll use the opportunity to announce the union of our little sister and the sheriff of Y Knot." Luke raised his glass again. "It took you long enough, Crawford," he said with a big grin. "Good thing I'm the forgiving type."

"I just wonder how Francis is going to feel about this." Chance had been quiet; now his eyes fairly twinkled. A roar of laughter went up at the mention of the ranch's youngest cowhand, who had been sweet on Charity since before he'd grown facial hair.

"He'll be brokenhearted, I'm sure," Mark added. "He's been dogging our sister's heels forever."

Charity laughed along with the rest of them, but her heart wasn't convinced. Brandon and the peculiar look in his eyes had her rattled.

Chapter Four

Luke helped Faith out of the wagon by the silvery light of a full moon, and then walked behind as they headed for the front door. Five-month-old Holly was wrapped in a blanket and snuggled against his chest. After the eventful evening at Cattlemen's, they'd gone by the big house, picked up the children, and made the ten-minute wagon ride out to their new home situated on top of a knoll in the south pasture. In the moonlight, the landscape was beautiful. It never failed to lift Luke's soul.

He stopped and glanced around. The dark shape of the new barn, a hundred feet away, loomed in a handful of trees. Life was blessed. Not that many years ago he'd felt the outcast, even in his own family. A half-breed trying to prove himself with every breath he took. Then Faith came into his life to buff away his hard edges. It was as if she'd been in his heart all along, tucked away in some secret recess, loving him.

"You coming, slowpoke?" Faith called softly from the front door.

She'd worn a pretty green dress tonight that complemented her caramel-colored eyes. Tendrils of her swept-up mahogany hair had fallen, giving her a tousled, come-hither look that never failed to stir his blood. Three-year-old Dawn was asleep in her arms.

Colton stood at her side, holding the baby's sack.

"What do you see?" she asked.

"More than I could have ever hoped for," he replied as he came forward. "I see a family where there was once a lonely man. The summer you showed up, my life changed. And our struggles are what led me to the truth about my real father."

After his mother's revelation that starry night at the horse corral, he'd shared the secret with Faith, knowing she'd keep it safe. It would be impossible not to tell her the reason why he'd been set free of his demons. His mother's admission lived in his heart, where he revisited it often.

He stopped and kissed her cheek.

"Is that all?" she asked.

"Ma, I'm going to bed," Colton interrupted, probably used to his parents' long conversations. His clothes were rumpled and his light brown hair mussed.

"Of course," Faith replied. She kissed him and traced a little cross on his forehead. "Sleep with the angels, sweetheart."

"Good night, son," Luke said. "We'll get that saddle on War Bonnet tomorrow. He's just being obstinate, sort of like his owner."

A crooked smile pulled at Colton's lips. "Good night, Pa," he said sleepily.

At ten, Colton had grown a whole four inches this year, but his voice had yet to drop. Luke's nephew Billy's had, much to Colton's dismay. Luke could tell it bothered his adopted son. Colton and Billy had a standing competition—all good-natured, of course, but still it was there.

Careful not to wake Holly in his arms, Luke closed the front door gently.

At the foot of the stairs, Faith turned. "I'll get this sleepy girl to bed," she said, rocking Dawn, whose head rested on her shoulder. The toddler's eyes were closed fast and her mouth looked like a little O as she dreamed. "And then I'll be back and feed Holly. Do you mind holding her for a few more minutes, Luke? Can the horses wait?"

"Do I ever grow tired of cuddling my little girl?" He'd learned the hard way to keep his voice down. Holding and rocking was much easier than dealing with a fussy cherub who'd had a few minutes of rest and was too wound up to fall back to sleep.

"The team will be fine. They've probably already fallen asleep in the harness."

"Thank you."

With Faith and Colton gone, he walked around the living room, a sense of pride filling him as he took the place in. He laid Holly on the sofa for half a minute while he lit two lanterns. The room was still a bit bare, but the essentials were all there since they'd completed construction a year ago. He admired the large logs he'd gathered on his own that spanned the length of the living room ceiling. The room, much smaller than the home he grew up in, felt cozy and spacious at the same time. He and Faith had gone into Bozeman to order some furniture, but the place still echoed a bit, needing a few paintings and rugs. All in good time, he thought, all in good time.

"I'm back," Faith called, coming down the stairs. Her face, full of love, was a sight he never grew tired of seeing. Finding her in that dilapidated old wagon had been the luckiest day of his life. She took Holly from his arms.

"Are you going to feed her out here?" He looked around the room.

She nodded. "I thought I would. In the chair by the window."

He followed her over and sat on the end of the brown sofa closest to her. She undid the buttons at her bodice, and when she was ready, opened up some of Holly's warm blankets and gave her a little jiggle. She fanned her hand in front of the sleeping baby to draw cool air across her face. It took several tries before the infant was awake enough to take what her mother was offering.

"What do you think about the big news tonight?" Faith said, once she'd settled in. "I'm sure you weren't surprised."

A smile lifted his mouth. "Not at all. Pleased—but wary too. I kind of wish Mother hadn't insisted on the month. You know them as well as I do. A lot could happen between now and then."

"Oh, certainly not, Luke. They've put those childish days behind them. I could tell by the way they looked at each other. Has your father said anything more about the acreage near town?"

"No. But I'm sure that will be something we touch on tomorrow. He's done a fine job of keeping Charity from the truth about the land we're donating to Y Knot for development. Ten of those acres will go to the town and the other fifty will go to Brandon and Charity. That way, she'll be able to start building a ranch of her own, as well as keep her hand in running the Heart of the Mountains. Brandon will be close enough so that it won't put a strain on his being sheriff. It's been a miracle she hasn't caught on sooner."

Faith sighed. She leaned over and kissed the top of Holly's head as she nursed. "It will be a wonderful surprise."

"I hope so. Until they say 'I do,' this lump in the pit of my stomach isn't going away. What Charity needs is one or two of those." He gestured to Holly. "To finally be good and married."

Faith gave him a stern look. "Is that what you think of me, Luke McCutcheon? A settled old mare with no kick left to surprise you?"

He jerked up straight. "No! Not at all," he hurried to say. Faith was never predictable—far from it. He looked for ways to keep her happy and content.

Faith laughed softly. "Good. You better say that." She gazed down at Holly and caressed her hair. "Charity will be a good mother, but not until she's ready. I sort of agree with you on wishing they'd tied the knot tonight. But since it didn't happen, I'm looking forward to the barn party and announcing the news to anyone who hasn't yet heard—not many, I'm sure. This month will prove to be long with all of us on pins and needles."

"We'll just have to make sure nothing derails their plans. Maybe you can spread the word with Rachel and Amy, and I'll do the same with Mark and Matt."

A soft tap on the door disturbed their conversation.

Faith's eyes widened. "Who could that be at this time of night?"

Luke stood and went to the door. "Who's there?"

Even on the ranch, one had to be careful at night. Most Indians were peaceful, but an occasional renegade still made trouble now and then.

"Roady."

Luke opened the door after Faith covered up with Holly's small blanket.

"I'm sorry to barge in this late," Roady began, looking back and forth between Luke and Faith. He removed his straw hat, holding it in his hands. "All the windows at the big house were dark, so I rode over here. Since the buckboard is still out front and your lights burning, I didn't think you'd mind." He motioned to the two lanterns, one on the rock mantel and another on the supper table.

"Of course we don't mind. Come in." Luke opened the door wide and gestured for their top cowhand to enter. Roady's rumpled denims and solid blue shirt had seen a long day's work. A black neckerchief was tied around his neck.

He stepped into the room but stayed on the small rug, mindful of his dirty boots. "I don't mind putting the wagon up when I leave."

"No, thanks. I'm on my way out just as soon as Faith puts Holly to bed. We were talking about Brandon and Charity. They finally announced their intention to marry. That move has been a long time coming. I guess Brandon finally got her to say yes out in Texas."

Roady grinned. "Glad to hear it. I'll go into town tomorrow and buy Brandon a beer. Taking on your little sister is no small feat."

"Hey," Luke warned good-heartedly.

"Knowing those two, I'm sure they have a surplus of humorous anecdotes to tell about John and Rio Wells."

"And some not so humorous," Faith said softly. "I'm amazed at the trouble Charity can get herself into—and out of—without even trying."

"With Brandon's help," Luke and Roady said at the same time.

Roady chuckled and cuffed Luke on the shoulder. They still stood by the door.

"What's your news that couldn't wait until morning?"

"Pedro found two steers with lumpy jaw in the second heifer pasture. He roped 'em and drug 'em back to the ranch, and put 'em in a separate corral at the main house. That was late this afternoon."

"What's lumpy jaw?" Faith asked.

"A condition the cattle can get in the soft tissue around their molars," Luke said. "If they have a puncture or wound from eating foxtails or rough forage, infection can set in. If it goes untreated, it'll fester, and the infection will spread to the other cattle from pus on the ground as they graze. Usually a treatment of iodine is all it takes to knock it out."

"But if it's let go," Roady added, "the infection calcifies. Big ol' lumps form that feel like rocks. The poor critters can't breathe, can't eat, and soon it's a total loss."

Luke nodded, thinking of all the possibilities. "It usually happens in two- and three-year-olds that are losing their baby teeth. Still could affect the whole herd if we don't take some quick action."

Roady ran a hand over his tired face. "This is the first case I've heard of in Montana."

"Last year in Wyoming, it got serious enough to make the papers." Luke looked at Roady. "Pass the word to all hands that if they see any questionable stock, they're to bring 'em in. Anything they're not sure about, take to Mark's corral, and the affected animals to the sick corral at the home ranch. I'll let Pa know first thing, and we'll have a ranch meeting tomorrow afternoon in the bunkhouse."

"Got it." Roady secured his hat back on his head. He looked at Faith and smiled. "Sorry to interrupt your evening, Faith."

"That's never a problem, Roady. You know that."

"Good night, then." Roady turned and reached for the doorknob.

"You heading to bed?" Luke asked. He hadn't had a chance to stop by the bunkhouse and check the schedule for a few days. With completing the barn and then working Colton's new horse, life had been busy. Now, with the lumpy jaw appearing in the herd, life would get busier.

"Back to the bunkhouse."

Roady left and Luke closed the front door. Leaning to the side was the wooden bar that he'd drop into place just as soon as he dealt with the horses. Slowly, he reached out and touched the sturdy barrier, thinking how his ma had tried and failed to protect herself against her abductors all those years ago.

"What is it?" Faith asked.

When he looked over, a scrunch of worry marred her brow. She could read him like a book.

"Nothin'," he replied with a smile.

He crossed the room and sank back into the sofa. The sight of his pretty wife did little to replace the niggling sensation of trouble in his gut. As hard as he tried, tonight that was impossible to do.

Chapter Five

After seeing Charity off with her parents, Brandon made one more fast visit to the jail. Jack was gone. The lamp left burning in the window cast a lonely light around the brick room. The jubilation he'd expected to feel on his return was dampened by the envelope burning a hole in his back pocket. With the wedding announcement, the meal, and the evening that had sped by so quickly, he'd hardly had a chance to think about what the letter might mean with respect to his and Charity's life.

He went to the back of the room and pulled open the solid, steel-fortified door. Dank air stirred in the short hallway. Three jail cells lined the right side. Each had a cot and blanket, a wooden bucket for drunkards' vomit, and a chamber pot. Beyond the bar-lined window was a view of Half Hitch Street and the livery. A light winked on in the rustic two-story barn. June Pittman must still be working.

Restless and not yet ready to open the letter, he turned on his heel. June would fill him in on the comings and goings of the regular folk while he'd been away. It wasn't until he was across the street that a deep male voice drifted out from the livery. By June's girlish laughter and quick, teasing tone, this fella might be more to her than just an acquaintance.

His curiosity pricked, Brandon paused at the open double doors. His gaze swept the large straw-strewn barn. June sat on a stall divider, an unknown man standing a foot away. With all their talk, they hadn't noticed his arrival.

"Good evening," he said.

"Brandon!" June hopped down and rushed over to give him a hug. "Welcome home! It's darn good to see your face back in Y Knot!"

She was only chin high, so Brandon had to lean over to accomplish the embrace. "Thanks, June. Saw your light burning from the jail window, and wanted to come over and say hello."

June's visitor stayed where he was. He was tall and burly and had a head of thick, dark hair. Brandon had never seen the man before.

"When did you get back?"

"This afternoon. Just finished supper with the whole McCutcheon clan at Cattlemen's."

June stepped away, her hands still clutching his arms, and took stock. Silly as it was, his face warmed as if out in the sun.

"How's Charity?"

"Good. And, actually, we announced our intention to marry tonight. News will be all over town by tomorrow. Lenore Saffelberg waited on our table and heard everything. Not that it's a big secret or anything."

She pulled him in for another heartfelt hug. It was then the big fellow crossed the dirt floor and stood by her side, staking claim. Brandon couldn't miss the hitch in his gait, unusual for someone his age. The hard set to his jaw and narrowed eyes said he did not appreciate the hugs his girl was giving to the newcomer. Brandon hid his smile.

Turning, June gripped the fellow's forearm and pulled him forward. "Brandon, this is Morgan Stanford. Came to town in your absence and works out at the Klinkner mill. Morgan, this is our long-lost sheriff, Brandon Crawford. All the citizens of Y Knot are going to be more than happy he's finally returned."

"Glad to make your acquaintance," Morgan said, taking his outstretched hand. "Sheriff, you say?" Morgan Stanford's gaze noted the absence of any star pinned to his vest.

Brandon reached up and fingered the spot where his star usually sat. "Haven't had a chance to pin on my badge. But good to meet you. You're working for Hayden and Norman? That's a darn good job. You're lucky to land it."

June nodded. "That's because Morgan is family. His sister is Hayden's new wife. Morgan filled in when Norman's leg got broke when his steam contraption blew up and Hayden needed help." She gazed up at Morgan with a silly smile on her face. "There's a lot that's happened since you've been gone."

"So I keep hearing. Hayden's wife?" Brandon took off his hat and wiped his brow. "Are you kiddin' me? First Holcomb and now Klinkner. What in the blazes went on in my absence?" He stared into the rafters for several seconds. "Seriously, I'm dumbfounded."

"It all started with that advertisement that ran in the paper a few months back, springtime. The one about the mail-order brides. First, Chance sent for one. Then Ina liked Evie so much, she sent for one on the sly for Hayden. You should have seen it around here, Brandon. All heck broke loose."

Brandon went over to a stool and sat down. "I'm sorry, I just had to sit. What in God's name did Hayden do when he found out? I'm surprised he didn't send her back."

Morgan stiffened abruptly. "That's my sister you're talking about."

"Sorry. Forgot that fact. It's just that I know Hayden and he'd be the last person I'd figure to be set up with a woman."

June stepped between the two well-matched men and put a calming palm on Morgan's chest. Here was another reason to be dumbfounded. He'd never known the feisty blacksmith to have a relationship with anyone before.

"Heather is beautiful, Brandon. You'll know her when you see her by her glossy black hair. She looks a lot like Morgan, but prettier." She laughed, and the man finally cracked a smile. Maybe they would end up friends after all.

Brandon stood and secured his hat back on his head. This night was turning out to be darn entertaining. He'd make a visit out to the mill tomorrow morning and say hello to Ina and Norman. Hayden too.

"I best be on my way," he said. "I want to take a quick walk down the street before everyone heads for home." He shook Morgan's hand again. "I didn't mean any disrespect to your sister, Stanford."

Morgan Stanford's expression softened. He was as tall as Brandon and looked as if he'd been to the school of hard knocks, the same as him. "No harm done. I guess I'll see you, then."

"Good night, June."

She looked content, Brandon thought. Taking over her father's business after he'd passed on was the best thing for her. She seemed truly well suited to running the livery and forge, as well as living in Y Knot.

Why couldn't he do that? Just be satisfied with his position here? Especially now that Charity had finally agreed to be his wife.

Perhaps the letter in his pocket was a rejection of his application for deputy marshal. That would sure simplify his life if the decision were made for him. Hope for that and hope that he'd gotten the job warred for space in his heart. A deputy federal marshal. Something he'd visualized since the day he met James Timberlake, the marshal who'd caught and killed the man who murdered Brandon's parents. His parents dead—all for three dollars and a horse and buckboard. The outlaw would have killed Brandon too if his pa hadn't pitched him from the careening wagon.

He'd never told a soul about that, not even Charity. Still, after twenty-one years the memory remained raw and hurtful. Maybe if he'd been in the wagon when the outlaw finally brought it to a halt, Brandon would have been able to do something to save his parents. Maybe, but not likely. A kid against a killer like that wouldn't stand much of a chance. He'd never know now. That unanswerable question would go with him to the grave.

From that time on, Timberlake's name had been burned into Brandon's mind. He'd lost track of Timberlake for a while until reading his name in the newspaper in connection with the dissolution of the James-Younger Gang a few years back. The bond that should have belonged to Brandon's father, if he'd lived, now fell to the Missouri lawman.

When he found out Timberlake was hiring two new deputies, Brandon had written to him asking for the job. It was on a whim, one of the occasions when Charity was having nothing to do with him, and he was tired of his feelings being trampled on. She could run so hot and cold, but darn, he loved her for it.

When he'd learned she was off to some charm school in Denver, he knew something else must be up. And it was a good thing he'd followed her. Saved her from the Comancheros, and they'd finally committed their love to each other. A long time coming, but it was worth the wait.

He fingered the envelope in his pocket. This letter, and the job if it happened, would be a true test for them. That was stone-cold fact. He didn't like to think about what the outcome might be.

Chapter Six

A soft knock sounded on Charity's bedroom door. Finished with her nighttime toilette, she donned her favorite blue nightgown with the pretty lace trim, reached for her wrapper, and slipped it on. Her nerves, strung tight, were not going to let her get a moment's rest tonight. Since Texas, she was used to having Brandon close by. Now he was all the way in Y Knot, where she couldn't talk with him.

She frowned, thinking of his disquiet at dinner. Something was wrong. He was wrestling with something, she could feel it, sure as the air she breathed.

Knock, knock.

"One moment, Mother," Charity called, and moved to open the door.

Her mom stood in the hall, also dressed for bed. In her hands was the carved wooden tray from Charity's childhood. On it were two cups of tea and a small plate of cookies.

A feeling of home enveloped Charity.

Her mom smiled. "How did you know it was me?" She came into the room and set the tray on the bedside table.

"Because the house is big and lonely. Everyone's moved out. Who else would it be?" She hadn't meant to sound churlish, but this fear in the pit of her stomach wouldn't let her be. "How can you stand it?"

"Charity, what's bothering you? I felt it in the restaurant and your statement now has just confirmed my suspicions. This is not like you at all." Her mother took her hands into her own. "Can you tell me?"

"Something's wrong with Brandon. He's acting strange."

Her mother smiled and tilted her head. "This is a big step. You and Brandon have been dancing around it for years—and now that the day has almost arrived, you don't know what to think or how to act. I believe you're the one who's nervous, not him."

Charity sank down on her bed and her mother sat beside her.

"You make me sound like a two-year-old, upset over my dolly being snatched away. Of course I know how to act. I love Brandon. I never knew how much until I was locked away in that tiny cell with a rattlesnake—like I was in Rio Wells."

Charity took a long cleansing breath to settle her nerves.

"All I could think about was him, Mom, and about all the time I wasted playing games. Well, I'm through with all that. I want nothing more than to become his wife. I thought he wanted that also, until he jumped at your suggestion to wait. On our way back from Texas, we promised each other that once we arrived we wouldn't let anyone change our minds. The second you brought it up, he agreed. I think now that he's home, he's getting cold feet."

"Oh, I see." The color drained from her mother's face.

Her mother had heard the complaint, but she'd also heard the blame.

Charity rushed to squeeze her hand. "Please, I'm not blaming you, Mother. I'm just questioning Brandon's feelings for me—before it's too late. Maybe they aren't as strong as what I feel for him."

"There is always one who loves more than the other. That's true in every marriage. He loves you. I can tell by the look in his eyes when you speak with each other."

Another knock on the door brought them both up straight.

"Claire, Charity, what're you doing?" her father called through the door. "It's late and Claire should be in bed. We have lots of plans to make come morning."

The timbre of her father's voice triggered a surge of emotion. Before she could stop them, tears filled her eyes. "Nothing, Pa. Mother brought me a cup of tea so we could talk. That's all." She exchanged a glance with her mother.

He cleared his throat. "But I feel left out."

"Flood, you had plenty of private time with our sons before each one got married, and now it's my turn with Charity. This is girl talk. Tomorrow, I'm sure she'll take a nice long ride with you. See the ranch. You know how much she's missed it."

When her mother looked at her, Charity nodded.

"I'll be in bed when I'm in bed." A smile tugged at Claire's lips. "And not a moment before. I hope you understand."

A moment passed, then Charity heard him harrumph. "I do. And I'll be counting on that ride tomorrow, Charity. How 'bout we ride up to Covered Bridge? You used to like that when you were little."

"Sure, Pa, that sounds like fun." And it did.

"Fantastic," Claire said. "Now, off to bed with you and read your book. I'll blow out the lamp when I come in if you've fallen asleep."

"Fine. Good night, then, Charity. We're happy you're home."

Unable to stop herself, Charity went to the door and pulled it open. "Thank you, Pa," she said, slipping into his arms for a hug. "I'm glad to be home too." *I may be staying.*

His arms were strong and safe—and always chased away any fear she had. When she sighed, he drew her closer, as if instinctively he knew she was struggling with something.

He kissed her on the forehead, then set her away. "Charity?"

"She's tired, Flood. Anyone would be after days of travel in a stagecoach—and arriving to a large dinner. Our family can be overwhelming even without trying. Be off with you now."

"Our family is not overwhelming," he grumbled, then made his way toward their bedroom.

Charity quietly closed the door and went over to the tray. She handed one cup to her mother and took the other for herself, settling back on the bed. Bringing the cup to her lips, she took a drink and let the warm liquid soothe her anxieties. "Thank you for that. I don't think I could talk through this whole thing with Pa too."

Her mother sipped her tea. "I do believe what I told Flood. Some of this nervousness stems from what you've been through. Brandon shared with me in private your harrowing experience. You've downplayed it for us. Being kidnapped and almost killed is not something you can just brush away. You would have died if Brandon and John hadn't found you."

"And Dustin."

"Yes, and Dustin. Don't you see? That alone has thrown your perceptions off. Then the long travel. The engagement. What I'm asking is that you give it a few days before you sound the alarm. I know you, Charity. You're a very passionate young woman. You don't do anything halfway."

She stood and went over to Charity's vanity. Opening the middle drawer, she drew out Charity's pearl-handled hairbrush. "Would you like me to brush your hair?"

This time, tears did spill down Charity's cheeks. Her tenderhearted mother remembered how much she enjoyed the gesture of love. She set down her tea and took the seat in front of the mirror.

With soothing hands, her mother gently gathered her hair to the back and drew the brush through. "All I'm asking, sweetheart, is for you to give it a little time. After a few days, you won't even remember what was upsetting you."

Charity gazed into the reflection of her mother's wise eyes. Perhaps she'd made too much out of Brandon's behavior tonight. He'd been through a lot of emotional turmoil himself in Texas, just as she had. This was supposed to be the happiest moment of their lives.

Yes. She would take her mother's advice. For the first time in hours, Charity felt a smile blossom in her heart. Her beloved Brandon wouldn't do her wrong. He'd never lead her on or hurt her. Never.

Charity reached up and took her mother's hand, the brush still in her long hair. "Thank you, Mother. Now that I think about Brandon without the suspicion in my heart, I believe you're right. I love him so much. And he loves me."

She stood and curled into her mother's waiting arms, happy. *Only one month and Brandon and I will finally be man and wife. Only one month and we'll say our "I dos." That's not long to wait at all.* Warm tingles flittered through her. *Only one month…*

Chapter Seven

The street hadn't gotten any less dusty in his time away. Still too keyed up to go home, Brandon crossed the deserted road and stopped in front of the sheriff's office. The sun had gone and night was just around the corner. Oil lamps glowed in the shop windows.

His house. That was another thing that had troubled him. How would Charity take to living in town? The tiny place went to whoever held the sheriff's job. It had been fine for him all these years, but was barely the size of the large living room at the ranch. She'd assured him more than once that she didn't need the grandeur of the ranch. Brandon knew she believed that wholeheartedly, but saying and doing sometimes didn't end up being the same.

Anxiety needled his mind, but he decided he'd think about that later, after he had a better picture of the town and what had transpired in his absence. Y Knot was his responsibility—one he'd let go longer than he should.

Crossing the street, he passed Berta May's dark sewing shop and stopped in the entrance of the Hitching Post Saloon. Peering over the bat-wing doors, he noticed a few men he didn't recognize amidst the regulars in the dimly lit hall.

Abe, the bartender, saw him and waved him in. "I heard you were back, Sheriff. Come in and wet your whistle."

Brandon smiled and pushed through the doors. He strode up to the long mahogany bar and placed his boot on the brass footrest. "Good to see you, Abe. How's business?"

Abe leaned on the curved edge of the bar. The skinny man's red suspenders held up his pants, and a white apron circled his waist. "Pretty darned good." Abe looked around and nodded. "But as you know, I don't hold much stock in your deputy. If the McCutcheons hadn't been here on a couple of occasions, Jack woulda lost control of the place. It's mighty good you're back. I'll breathe easy now."

Brandon felt duly appreciated. "I'll make a point to stop by often so any cowboys looking for a high time will know I've returned. You had a lot of trouble?"

"Just when that mail-order bride got the men worked up. Then there was a shootout over a feller accused of dealing from the bottom."

"What happened?"

"Before Jack could get here—he's always a bit slow; that is, if you can find him—the two drunkards drew on each other. Both had a snoot full, so no one was kilt, just wounded. Doc Handerhoosen took the plugs out and stitched 'em up. A week later, they rode out of town together as if nothin' had happened."

Sometime during Abe's storytelling, a prickle crawled up Brandon's spine. He glanced discreetly in the large mirror. No one back there was paying him any mind. He glanced out the door, but the street was dark. He mentally shrugged the thought away.

"You want a beer, Sheriff? It's on the house."

Sated from dinner, wine, and the champagne as well, Brandon shook his head. He needed to get home and face whatever was in that letter. "No, thanks, Abe. But I appreciate the offer. I'll finish my walk around and get home. I'll take you up on your generous offer another time."

There it was again, making his nerves tingle. *I haven't stayed alive this long by ignoring my gut. Someone is watching me, and I want to know who.*

He turned. What had raised his suspicions? Every man in the room had his head down. Reading a fistful of cards, admiring his whiskey-filled shot glass, or asleep on the table. A sound made him glance at the stairs leading to the second floor. A beautiful woman stood on the halfway landing. When she was sure she had his attention, a seductive smile curled the corners of her strawberry lips.

"That's Fancy Aubrey, our new saloon girl," Abe said from behind him. "Arrived just after you left town."

Saloon girl? Didn't he mean woman? No miss in Brandon's lifetime had ever looked like *that*. A blue satin dress clung to her hourglass shape, and her blond hair was done up on her head, an abundance of curling tendrils framing her perfectly shaped oval face. Her chin was set just so, and her posture reflected years of practice. He could see the vivid blue of her eyes all the way from where he stood.

"Really." That was all he got out before the woman gracefully descended the stairs, glided across the scarred wood floor, and stopped at his side.

"Who's this handsome man, Abe?" she said, using her voice like a velvet weapon. She ran her hand down Brandon's arm as he took her stock. Her blue stone earrings glinted in the light of the lanterns against her powdered skin. "You new in town, sugar?"

Abe sputtered and reached out as if to personally take her hand from Brandon's arm. "This is Brandon Crawford, Fancy. Sheriff of Y Knot. And you best keep your hands to yourself or Charity McCutcheon may come in here and give you what for."

Amused, Brandon touched the brim of his hat. "Miss Aubrey. I'm pleased to make your acquaintance." He glanced at Abe. "I keep meeting all sorts of pretty ladies just come to town. Maybe I should leave more often."

"That must be Evie Holcomb you're referring to," Fancy said. "I saw her on the boardwalk this afternoon with that handsome husband of hers. That girl has a heart of gold. She can't understand why women cross to the other side of the road when they see me coming." Fancy laughed, but Brandon didn't miss the slight wobble in her lips.

"You and Chance's wife are friends?" He wasn't judging, just surprised.

"Yes, we are, Sheriff. Chance too, as a matter of fact. Does that shock you?"

Things are getting more interesting by the second. "Maybe."

The saloon doors swished open and Francis, the young cowhand who worked for Charity's family out at the ranch, came striding in. The seventeen-year-old's face brightened when he saw Brandon.

Brandon took a step away from Fancy Aubrey to put a decent amount of space between them, since she didn't seem so inclined. If anything, he'd felt her inching closer.

"Francis," Brandon said. He came forward and the two gripped hands. "It's darn fine to see you."

"You too, Brandon. I'd heard you and Charity arrived this afternoon." The color of Francis's face deepened, and he kept his eyes trained far away from the seductive saloon girl by Brandon's side.

"Aren't you going to say hello, Francis?" Fancy said in mock hurt. "You're breaking my little heart. I thought we had something nice going."

Francis stammered, then said, "Hello, Fancy. You sure look purty tonight."

She batted her lashes. "Thank you. I'm delighted you noticed. Abe, give Francis a beer on me."

Was that true? Did the two really have something going? She was years older than the lad.

Francis scuffed his boot nervously and brought his attention back to Brandon. "I'm here picking up a couple of horses from the livery. Threw some shoes." His clean face and slicked-back hair would be wasted on a couple of horses. Brandon also detected the warm, spicy scent of the aftershave Lucky made in the bunkhouse from rum boiled with bay leaves, cinnamon, lavender, and other odd spices. His way of combating the unpleasant aroma of manure-covered boots and dirty clothes.

"This late?"

"June knows I'm coming."

Abe set a foamy mug on the bar. "Here you go, son." The bartender looked speculatively at Brandon. "How's Charity doing? Word's got around town how she snuck down to Rio Wells to see John, and how you had to fetch her back. I'm sure Luke and the rest are plenty glad to put that fiasco to rest." Abe looked at Fancy when her shapely eyebrows lifted. "Charity is the youngest McCutcheon and only girl. She and Brandon..."

Fancy pursed her lips. "Are?"

"Engaged," Brandon supplied. Lenore and June knew. Tomorrow, the whole town would be talking.

Abe slapped the bar. "Congratulations, Sheriff! That's just dandy. We've had a bet going 'round to see if the two of you'd come back hitched, or fightin' again. Seems none of us were right. We'll have to roll that over into a new pot to bet on. I wish you both the best of luck."

Something in the man's eyes said they were going to need it. Brandon tried not to respond in anger. He supposed Y Knot's interest in his and Charity's relationship was understandable. They'd been putting on a show for years. At least out at the ranch, Charity didn't have to contend with the teasing every day like he did.

Francis picked up his beer and took a long guzzle. He'd been sweet on Charity for as long as Brandon could remember, unmindful of her being three years his elder.

"Congratulations, Brandon," Francis finally said. "Good luck and all that."

"We appreciate your good wishes, Abe, Francis. And it was my pleasure meeting you, Fancy Aubrey." He touched the brim of his hat. "If you need anything, just let me know. Or if anyone gives you a hard time, I want to hear about it. I like to keep Y Knot peaceful for everyone."

Fancy arched her back and gracefully placed a hand on her hip. "Thank you, Sheriff. I'll be sure to do just that."

Brandon had put off the correspondence from Kansas City for as long as he could. Trying doorknobs to be sure they were securely locked, he made his way down the boardwalk toward the sheriff's office and his small house out back.

What would the letter say? If he'd gotten the job, it would surely tip his chance with Charity right out the window. And if he hadn't gotten the job, he'd always wonder where his life could have gone if he had. Neither option seemed to satisfy. But knowing would put a rest to this endless questioning.

At the end of the alley behind his office, Brandon unlocked his door and pushed it open. Cool, musty air hit him in the face as he hung his black felt Stetson on a peg, then walked through the darkened room into the tiny kitchen, where he lit the lamp.

Home sweet home.

The simple domain wasn't much, but it was plenty enough for him. It had been his home for the past six years—and he liked it. He'd be lying if he said different. The place was clean and tidy. Extra pair of boots sat in the corner by the back kitchen door. Dishes clean and stacked on the counter; no sense using energy to put them in the cupboard when they were handier right there. One chair at the small, beat-up old wooden table. Yep, perfect for a one-man show.

Charity had only been inside once. She'd ridden into town with Luke and they'd come looking for him when the sheriff's office was empty. He'd been lounging in the front room, boots off, eating a plate full of beef and beans and a hank of fresh bread ripped from the loaf Berta May had baked him that morning. Charity had been thirteen and hadn't been able to mask her surprise at his small, threadbare bachelor pad.

Brandon chuckled, remembering her expression. Over the years, he and Luke had gotten many good laughs recalling the stunned surprise on his little sister's face. It didn't feel quite so funny anymore.

No more stalling. He pulled the envelope from his back pocket and scooted out the wooden chair. He opened the post. The salutation was brief, addressed to Brandon Crawford, Sheriff of Y Knot, Montana Territory.

I do indeed remember you, son! So many years have passed since that fateful and sad day that took the lives of both of your parents, that I dare say you probably will not recognize me. I have to say I am surprised to get this letter, but delighted as well. So, you are a lawman too. That stands to reason. Moreover, I am relieved I will not have to explain anything about the job to you—the dangers and the fact many lawmen do not reach their fiftieth birthday. I will make my final decision after I meet the men interested. Come to Kansas City by...

Brandon blinked, then looked away in deep thought. July 26th was only two weeks away. If he'd gotten the post when he should have, he would have had a good month and a half to break the news to Charity and plan the trip. As it was, he'd be lucky to make the appointment on time.

Luke's shindig was in a few days. Maybe he could pull together his travel plans and then speak with Charity the day before. He wouldn't spring it on her at the party. They'd need time alone to talk.

Brandon had never been to Kansas City. Images of streetcars and businesspeople going about their day filled his mind. Horses, men's clubs, telephones...all the things he'd read about in the Y Knot *Sunday Herald*. Perhaps it would be like San Antonio, bustling with activity.

Maybe he was blowing this all out of proportion. Charity had liked her time in Rio Wells. Said how much she enjoyed the travel and experiencing how the rest of the country lived. Would she consider accompanying him to the interview? Excitement warmed Brandon's insides. No—better yet, they could marry first. Make it a true honeymoon.

He smiled—a real smile—for the first time since Jack had handed him the letter. What was the saying about having one's cake and eating it too? It could happen. Charity had grown up so much on this last trip. With the way she'd pledged her love to him over and over, there was no way she wouldn't be as happy as he was for this big chance.

What the devil was he thinking? Nothing ever went as planned when it came to Charity. She was a force to be reckoned with, and then some. Maybe that was why he loved her so much. She kept him on his toes. Even if this was his big break, predicting her response was iffy, at best. He could suggest eloping to Missouri, but after agreeing to Mrs. McCutcheon's request for a month, going back on the word he'd given only hours before felt wrong. He'd hate to anger his mother-in-law and start the marriage off on the wrong foot.

What to do? There didn't seem to be an answer that would make everyone happy. More likely, the opposite would happen, leaving a trail of broken hearts. And losing Charity would break his heart most of all.

Chapter Eight

Charity fairly flew down the long staircase to find her mother and father alone at the dining room table. "Good morning," she sang happily.

"Good morning, dear," her mother replied. "I can see that you slept well. Was it good to be back in your own bed?"

Her father set his cup in his saucer as he waited for her reply.

"Did I. And yes, it was. I opened my window and all the fresh air had me feeling like a baby. I'm so well rested and ready to make plans for the wedding. Mother, your suggestion to wait was a good one. I'll only have one wedding and one opportunity to plan. The next few days will be fun."

"Well, whatever you and your mother talked about last night made all the difference," Flood said. "When I retired, I was a little worried that you were having second thoughts."

"Never," Charity said quickly, drawing a look from her father. "I can't wait to marry Brandon. He is everything to me. I want to have a big family, just like you two."

Esperanza came into the room carrying a plate and the coffeepot. "I hear your voice, Miss Charity." She smiled and set the ham and eggs in front of Charity, then filled her coffee cup. "I will be right back with some juice and cream for your coffee."

"Thank you so much, Esperanza. You're a jewel."

Claire laughed. "How I wish I could bottle your enthusiasm."

Unable to wait for the cream, Charity took a drink of the aromatic coffee. "I was thinking of riding into town today—" She raised her hand when Claire opened her mouth to object. "Just to see Brandon for three minutes. We were together so much in Texas, even one day feels like torture without him."

Flood leaned forward, his eyes narrowing. "How together were you?"

She tamped back a jab of irritation. "Not together like *that.*"

Flood sat back and reached for his coffee cup. "That's a relief."

Claire quieted him with a look, then directed her attention back to her daughter. "You do what you want, but if it were me, I'd give him some time to miss you. Absence makes men's hearts grow fonder. It's true."

Flood nodded. "Your mother knows what she's talking about. He'll be swamped with business for a few days—and your appearance might not have your desired effect. Let him get settled and back in his routine. It's not that he won't want to see you, but he's a very steely young man. He takes his responsibilities seriously, like everyone should."

And then some, Charity thought. Brandon was a lawman through and through. *Something I love about him very much.* She cut her ham and ate a slice. When Esperanza returned with a glass of orange juice and a small pitcher of cream, Charity doused her coffee with a more-than-generous dollop and added a teaspoon of sugar. *It's so wonderful to be home.*

She swallowed her food, then took another drink of her doctored-up coffee. "Maybe you're right. And the party is only three days away. Yes, I'll concentrate on plans, visit Faith, Rachel, and Amy to get their ideas. May I wear your wedding dress, Mother?"

"I had hoped you'd ask. I'll send one of the hands into town today to ask Berta May to come out for a fitting in the next few days. I'm sure there won't be much that has to be done to it. I was your size when I married your father."

Charity stood, her plate half eaten.

Her father blinked in surprise. "Where're you going? You just sat down. You haven't finished your breakfast yet."

"I can't take another bite. I have too many things to do—and I'm not hungry at all."

Claire put out a hand in an effort to stop her. "But—"

"But nothing," Charity replied. "I'm going out to the bunkhouse. I want to see Lucky and the boys and tell them the news personally before anyone else does."

Her parents laughed, and Charity couldn't remember another time when they'd both looked so pleased about something she was up to. Usually she was in trouble, and one parent, after her petitionary begging, was assuaging the other on her behalf. Charity liked this new leaf. She liked being on their good side. She liked the love she saw written plainly on their faces.

Charity knocked on the bunkhouse door, then gripped her hands in front of her buckskin riding pants, trying to be patient. The ranch yard looked neat and clean, the same horses stood in the corral as when she'd left, the same sunshine streamed through the branches of the tall pine trees. An array of branding irons decorated the sidewall next to the door. When she was little, the sight fascinated her for hours. Each brand was a story in itself.

As the only girl in the family, she'd been strictly forbidden to enter the bunkhouse without permission from Lucky—and only Lucky. It was the cowhands' domain. They deserved privacy after long hours in the saddle. This was the only rule she'd been smart enough to know there would be hell to pay if she broke, and she never had.

A barrage of lively voices inside meant the men were up and eating, and perhaps hadn't heard her first request to come in. She knocked again, this time with the heavy horseshoe knocker in the middle of the door. Just as she was about to give it another go, the door opened and she smacked Lucky in the face.

Surprised, the bunkhouse cook grabbed his nose and yelped.

She let out a cry of dismay and snatched back her hand.

"Lucky, I'm so sorry!" She put her arm around his middle and they walked a few feet into the bunkhouse.

Chairs scraped back as all the men stood. "Miss Charity!" A surge of warm happiness squeezed Charity's heart.

"Let me see," she pleaded, still trying to see Lucky's face. She pried his hands down. "I hope I didn't give you a bloody nose." Relieved when there was no blood in sight, she let go her held breath.

He blinked several times and scrunched his nose. "No harm done, Miss Charity," he said, wiggling it around, and then feeling it with his fingers. "Welcome home."

"I'm sorry to barge in on you like this." She was unable to keep her smile from her face. These men had practically raised her. She loved each and every one. "Please sit down and finish your breakfast before your flapjacks get cold. I just wanted to be the first to tell you—Brandon and I are *finally* getting married. You're all invited."

A happy cheer went up. Lucky pulled her into an embrace. "That's darn good news, honey bear. We're all tickled pink."

One by one, the cowhands sat back down at the long rectangular table filled with food. A platter of potatoes, mixed with red onion and chilies, was next to a large bowl of scrambled eggs. Toast was piled a mile high, and every plate already had a flapjack or two. A red-and-white plaid napkin hung from each man's collar, whether he was dressed for the day or was still rumpled from sleep. Roady Guthrie, shaved and spit shined, smiled at her and nodded. The hand they called Uncle Pete, even though he was no relation, still had a chin full of whiskers. John Berg and Smokey finally swallowed what they'd been chewing before she'd barged in, and wiped their mouths with a napkin. Francis stood out like a sore thumb. His mouth, stretched tight in a line, and his eyes, a cool, frosty gray as he regarded her, made her uneasy.

Charity took them in. "You already knew? I can tell by your expressions."

Lucky nodded. "Yep. I can't fib to ya. Roady came back from Luke's last night with the good news. But it don't matter who tells us, just that the event is happening. When's the day?"

"As soon as we can pull together all our plans. Probably a month, or sooner. We would have done it last night, but Mother wanted some time to plan a wedding, me being her only daughter."

Francis stood back up. He took the napkin from his neck and dropped it beside his plate. "I told 'em too, Miss Charity. Even before Roady did. I ran into Brandon last night in the saloon, *talking* with Fancy Aubrey." He raised his eyebrows, as if wanting to make sure she grasped his meaning—that it was more than just talk.

A hush fell across the room like a wet blanket on a newborn pup. Who was Fancy Aubrey? And why was Brandon speaking with her?

"I tried to get a word in edgewise, you know, to ask about *you,* but they were in some deep conversation and didn't see me for several minutes. I never did find out what was so all-important that the rest of us couldn't hear." He shrugged. "Oh well. Guess we'll never know."

Francis glanced around at the men's pinched looks, and even from where Charity stood, she could see the top of his ears turn pink.

She lifted her chin, hurt that Francis would want to wound her this way. Her more sensible side cautioned against believing his words, even though a warm sensation crept up her neck as she pictured any woman doting on her man. And Brandon? Was he interested?

"Well, I'm sure he was glad you stopped in, Francis—when you finally caught his attention, that is. He never has anything but nice things to say about you whenever we talk. Thinks of you as family."

Some men kept their gazes on their plates and others looked like they wanted to skin Francis alive. She felt Lucky's hand on her shoulder.

"You pull up a chair and squeeze in between John and Smokey," he said firmly. "I'll fix ya a plate of flapjacks, just the way you like 'em—drowning in sweet butter and maple syrup. I have the batter right here and the skillet hot. Why, when you was a little tyke, you'd beg me to make 'em practically every week. 'Lucky,' you'd say in that sweet little-girl voice. 'I ain't had your flapjacks in a month of Sundays,' and it had only been just the week before you said the same thing. You'd smile at me with a gap-toothed grin, and I'd melt like butter. I made 'em, sure enough, and was happy ta do it."

All the men chuckled.

Charity struggled to keep her smile in place.

Francis stepped away from the table and went over to his bunk at the far end of the room, where he took his black leather vest from a peg over his bed. He drew the garment on, then sat on his cot as if he didn't want to hear her stories.

"I've already eaten inside, Lucky, but thank you. You always did make the best flapjacks this side of the Rockies. Esperanza filled my plate with so much food, you'd think she thought I hadn't eaten since I'd left the ranch."

"That's good," Lucky replied affectionately. "You could use a little fattening up. But that don't mean ya can't have some coffee and visit with us." He gimped over to the stove and filled a mug halfway with dark liquid, then poured cream to the brim. "You're not getting out of here without telling us all about Rio Wells and John and his new wife—so stop thinking ya can. We've been waiting impatiently." He handed her the cup and guided her over to a chair.

"Please, Miss Charity," Roady said. "We really do want to hear." Smokey and the others nodded.

"That's right. Three months is a long time." Uncle Pete scratched his whiskered cheek. "I'll bet you have lots to tell."

Charity took a deep breath, unwilling to let any of the hands see how much Francis's words had shaken her. They shouldn't, she chided herself. She trusted Brandon. He was the sheriff. It was his job to check on the people, all the people, of Y Knot. Saloon girls included.

But that didn't mean she couldn't meet this woman too, and let her know Brandon was spoken for.

Chapter Nine

Fox Dancing wiped the water droplets from her mouth, rolled to her feet, and stood, surveying the land. She'd never been this far south. The dull ache in her stomach reminded her that her dried meat was gone and she'd have to start hunting if she wanted fresh. Right now, foraging for berries and roots would have to do, regardless that those were considered old-woman's food. She'd be grateful to have them.

The sharp cry of an eagle pulled Fox Dancing out of her musing. She climbed the bank of the pebble-strewn beach and walked to her Appaloosa mare. Searching the afternoon sky, she spotted the eagle overhead, a small black speck in the clouds.

A good sign.

She smiled. The Great Spirit was watching out for her safety. Would make her journey successful. Bring her to her brother's dwelling, where she'd see him with her own eyes.

Luk Macatceen's legend in their village had grown as the years passed. Her two mothers had spread the good medicine her father had shared with them about him, her powerful half-white brother. The white woman, Luk's mother, had been bartered for return many moons after she'd been given to her father. Her white husband had come with a string of fine horses, so many that no man would have been able to turn them down. To avoid bloodshed, her father had agreed, and delivered his third wife back into the hands of her white husband, but not before he'd been told in a dream that she was carrying his son. A very powerful son. He'd hated to relinquish her, but he could see in her eyes from the moment she heard the name Macatceen, she'd never really been his to keep.

Her father had traveled this route several times to see his half-white son, never thinking she'd one day do the same.

Now it was her turn to see her brother. What would Luk Macatceen do when he saw her? Would he recognize the slant to her eyes and the high set to her cheekbones as his? Their father said she held a strong resemblance to him. Excitement surged within when she thought of the meeting. It was fortunate Luk's mother had taught her father some of the white language, which he'd passed on to Fox Dancing.

Well, she'd never get there if she stood around daydreaming about him. She took out her knife and dug at the base of a reed, pulling up a stalk with three tubers attached to the root. She continued until she had a handful, then went back to the stream to wash them in the sparkling cold water.

Taking a bite, she chewed, wishing the rubbery root was a fresh slice of elk meat, hot from the coals.

Men's voices drifted across the water to where she stood.

Instantly, she dropped to her stomach.

She flattened herself out on the cold ground, her heart jerking wildly, painfully in her chest. Glancing over to her horse, asleep on the bank, she spotted her quiver and bow where she'd left them on a rock.

Where were they? She picked up her head just enough to scan the opposite side of the stream. Blood pulsed in her ears, making it difficult to hear anything else. So far from home, they were sure to be white. Being caught would mean a slow and dishonorable death—one she was not ready to face.

She dragged in a raspy breath, praying her horse didn't nicker when she heard the other animals approaching.

Through narrowed eyes, Fox Dancing spotted the riders. Not far, and coming in her direction. Leather cases hung from their saddles, carrying steely gray rifles.

If she didn't go now, she'd be found. She was surprised they hadn't seen her already.

Fox Dancing pushed to her feet. Before the men even saw her, she'd gathered her weapons and vaulted onto her mare.

A shout went up.

She recognized the word *Indian*, then the word *squaw*. She had her mare turned and into a full gallop before she dared to glance over her shoulder.

With gleeful faces, the white men were charging across the stream at the same time they reached for their rifles. Leaning onto the neck of her mare, she flung back her arm, slapping her horse's flank with her bow.

Her mare surged forward. Pulling the leather rein, Fox Dancing guided her horse sharply to the left and ascended a steep embankment that the white dogs would never be brave enough to ride. She clung to her mare's long mane, squeezing with her legs when she felt herself slipping back.

Trees and rocks blocked her path, impeding her getaway. Her mare slowed, heaving beneath her as she struggled to make the climb.

The crashing sound behind told her the men were still giving chase. Laughter reached her ears, then a curse. A bullet zipped past her head and splintered a branch next to her face.

Had she fled Painted Bear Stone just to be dishonored at the hands of white dogs and then killed?

She wouldn't consider that option! She'd meet her white brother. She'd seen the meeting in a dream.

Her horse, breathing hard, finally crested the embankment. Fox Dancing took heart. She could now kill the men hunting her with ease, if she chose to. But that would only bring more white dogs sniffing after her trail.

With a bloodcurdling cry, she spun her horse toward the dense forest and disappeared inside. She was surprised to still hear the men in pursuit. Turning to look one more time, she didn't see the slick black ferns of a woodland spring until it was too late. Her mare slipped, going down. An upturned branch impaled Fox Dancing's arm.

She swallowed her cry of pain. Moisture sprung to her eyes as her horse scrambled to her feet. On her hands and knees, Fox Dancing emptied the little contents of her stomach onto the musty earth floor. Taking several deep breaths, she grasped the branch sticking out of her arm and yanked it out. She climbed to her feet, a wave of dizziness almost dropping her.

I am a fierce warrior. Nothing can sto—

She blinked, clearing her blurred vision and foggy mind. Large leaves and branches hid her for now, but it wouldn't be long before the men found her.

I won't die like this!

She fingered the knife sheathed in leather and tied around her waist, remembering the stories of women who had used theirs to keep from being dishonored. Sweat slicked her forehead. She dug through her pack for the soft skin wraps she'd packed, then clumsily bandaged her arm to stop the bleeding.

All the while, the men kept coming.

She swayed. Gulping in breaths, she wrapped her fists in her mare's mane, and with a cry of agony, pulled herself onto the mare's back, praying for strength to say mounted.

Chapter Ten

The hour in the bunkhouse with the cowhands had been just what Charity had needed. She hadn't laughed so much in years. And she'd been able to put Francis's comment out of her mind. He was hurt. He'd staked claim on her years ago, whether she wanted it or not. She'd tried often enough to let him know he was just a friend, but maybe now that the time had come for her and Brandon, he was taking it harder than expected.

When her father and brothers arrived to begin the day's work, she saddled up and rode over to Rachel's. Faith and Amy were already there, children in tow. She spent the rest of the morning playing with her darling nieces. She and her sisters-in-law had planned the visit last night at Cattlemen's, and while she would have loved to sit in on the bunkhouse meeting to hear how they would combat the lumpy jaw Pedro had discovered, she didn't want to renege on yesterday's promise.

Riding back into the ranch yard on her palomino, Charity arrived just as the door to the bunkhouse opened and everyone streamed out. Eight horses were tied at the hitching rail, and a scattering of hens pecked at the dirt between their feet.

"Charity," Flood called. "You ready to ride? We're going to Covered Bridge and Three Forks."

She waved, then rode up next to Luke, Matt, Mark, Roady, and her father. The rest of the men mounted up and headed out. "I'm ready and able. I haven't ridden the pastures for months. I miss it."

"Well, it's good you're back, because we can use your help," Luke said. "We're riding in pairs to check the stock. If you find any infected animals, bring 'em back here so we can treat 'em with iodine. Another set of eyes will be useful."

Flood gathered his reins and mounted, as agile as any of her brothers.

"How come you get to go with Charity, Flood?" Roady asked, a teasing light in his eyes.

Flood gave him a stern look. "Because it's been months since I had a ride with my daughter. She's getting married soon, so the opportunities will be few and far between. Especially after she has a little Brandon or Charity."

Charity could hardly believe her ears. Embarrassed, she turned her head, and her brothers and Roady laughed.

"You better get used to it," Matt said. "Once you're a married woman, you'll hear all sorts of new things."

"If you say so."

Matt winked at her. "I just did. Hey, how was the tea party? Rachel could hardly sleep last night with excitement. She had me dig out her best linen and set up an extra little table for the tykes, all before you arrived."

When Charity heard that, she was doubly glad she hadn't canceled time with the family to join the meeting.

"It was nice. Her berry pie was delicious. And before you ask—there's plenty left for you."

"Thank goodness. The smell of it baking this morning about drove me loco."

As Flood loped away, he called over his shoulder, "You coming, Daughter, or are you going to sit there all day talking?"

It took a good twenty-minute lope to make it out to the big herd. Luke and Mark would be out to check this group, but she'd asked her pa if they could come this direction on their way to Covered Bridge so she could see the sight of all those steers grazing. The vision always did funny things to her insides.

They stopped on a hill overlooking a valley filled with bovine. "You know, Pa, I really enjoyed Texas, but I'll never be able to describe how much I missed this."

She swung her arm wide, indicating the land and the cattle.

"You don't have to explain anything to me, darlin'. I understand completely. And I wasn't even born here. You were. This land is in your blood. I don't think you could get it out even if you tried."

They sat for a few minutes in silence, just enjoying the view.

"Have you and Brandon discussed where the two of you will live? Will you stay in his house in town?"

Flood tipped his hat back and turned to her, a totally innocent look on his face.

Charity fought to keep a straight face. A year ago, while she was in Y Knot, she'd stopped into the office of Mr. Browning, attorney-at-law, and the man who represented the ranch if they had need of counsel. Everyone had been out to lunch. She had a parcel from her father to deliver, so she put it on the man's desk. She wasn't snooping, but right there, for all the world to see, was a document labeled LAND GIFT FOR CHARITY McCUTCHEON. With a heading like that, it would have been impossible not to stop and glance it over.

Her parents and brothers were gifting her, upon her marriage, a chunk of land she and Brandon could build on, make into whatever they chose. She knew they'd done it so Brandon would be close enough to town to keep an eye on things as sheriff, and yet live with her where she'd be happy— and where she'd be nearer to the home ranch so she could continue to work there.

"Where else? For now, at least, I'll move into his house behind the sheriff's office. I admit, it'll be different, a huge change for me, but I'm looking forward to it. A little variation is always good, don't you think, Pa? At least, that's what you've always said."

"Indeed."

He was looking at the cattle again. She loved when his eyes took on that faraway, dreamy look, and his lips turned up, resembling her brothers'.

"That's what brought me out to Montana all those years ago," he said. "And gave me the inspiration to leave the rest of my brothers behind and see what life had to offer over the next rise. As much as I've missed them through the years, I wouldn't change a thing about my life."

She almost sighed at his intense countenance. He was thinking back, remembering all the good times.

"It was in this rugged, take-no-prisoners land that I met your mama. My whole life changed." He chuckled and shook his head. "Your grandfather was dead set against her marrying a thick-skulled hothead—that's what he used to call me. His sweet girl was the apple of his eye and his only child. We met on a frigid December night when the snow swirled so thick I couldn't see the hand in front of my face."

He removed his hat and scratched his head. "From the moment I saw Claire, I knew she was the one I would marry. I was smitten. Couldn't think of anything or anyone but her. Her pa knew I wouldn't give up, so after a month he finally said yes—but that we'd have to wait three months." He chuckled again and gazed off at the cattle, deep in thought.

"Well, what happened?" Charity asked. "You're not stopping there."

"What happened?" he repeated. "I worked every job I could find, and that was no easy feat because Y Knot was hardly even a town back then. Jobs were few and far between. I scraped together what little money I could and built her a small one-room log cabin, then began building this ranch, one steer at a time."

"And the boys?"

"They started coming along faster each year, and finally you. As much as Claire loves her sons, which she does with all her heart, when you surprised us, something inside her blossomed. It was as if after having four sons in a row, she hadn't believed a daughter was possible."

He reached over and patted her leg, making her throat squeeze tight.

"We're going to miss you, darlin', and that's a fact I'm not ashamed to say out loud to the whole world."

"Pa, stop. You're making me all sentimental. I'm not going anywhere—far, at least."

He reined around. "You better not. So just humor me a little. You'll understand better when your last ragamuffin is ready to fly the coop." His voice became thick, and he pulled his hat low. "Come on, we have work to do." He urged his mount into a jog, headed east.

Charity followed. "That's a lifetime away, Pa," she called. "I want to enjoy my youth for a while before I start bemoaning a nest empty of children I don't even have."

"You better prepare yourself. Life goes by faster than you think—and takes some unexpected turns along the way."

Thirty minutes later, they arrived at Covered Bridge. Charity's mare put her head down and snorted when Charity asked her to cross, but followed tentatively after Flood's horse.

The rushing water made a cheerful sound and the air was cool and inviting. After crossing, they halted on the other side of the river. "Where do you think the cattle are?" she asked.

"This way. Usually they're in the valley by the aspen grove." Without another word, they loped off.

As usual, her pa was right. It was a smaller herd of about seventy-five head, but it would take a good part of the day to ride through them all.

"Okay, Daughter, we'll start here and ride about fifteen feet apart. Let's go."

Charity made her way slowly into the bawling herd, her cutting horse well versed in the action. Nervously, the cattle fanned out at a trot, opening a path. She halted and let the cattle settle. They stopped and looked at her. Several dropped their heads back to eat, while others still eyed her suspiciously.

When they were calm, she took a few slow steps. She was close enough that she could reach out and touch some if she were so inclined. With a keen eye, Charity did a quick study of each heifer's face, looking for any sign the animals had problems eating or breathing. In advanced stages of lumpy jaw, the heifer would be weak and unsteady on her feet.

"See anything?" Flood called over.

"Nothing yet. But I sure love the smell of these cattle. It's good to be ranching."

She swatted a fly out of her face and her thoughts meandered to the bunkhouse and how much she loved the hands. Then to Francis and what he'd said.

Who was Fancy Aubrey anyway? Even only hearing the elaborate saloon-girl-sounding name once, it was firmly branded in her mind, never to be forgotten. Surely, with a name like that, she was beautiful. Sultry. Sexy. Totally tempting to a man like Brandon. And totally the opposite of Charity's tomboy ways.

A heifer in front of Charity lifted her tail and made a perfectly round splat of cow dung on the ground.

Brandon liked self-assured women. Ones who could take care of themselves as good as any man. Didn't he?

Two hours passed in the hot sun, making her chaps feel all the heavier on her legs. Almost finished with this herd, Charity reached for her canteen and took a mouthful of cool water.

Riding slowly forward, she spotted an unusually short heifer in front of her that had her nose to the ground but wasn't eating. Listlessly, the bovine turned her head and glanced in Charity's direction, but didn't trot away.

"I think I've got one over here, Pa," she shouted through cupped hands. "I'll bring her out."

Charity took her rope and shook out the loop. With very little effort, because the cow was so close and didn't seem to have the volition to run off, she landed her loop nicely over the animal's head. Charity dallied her rope around her horn and started for the edge of the herd, where her pa was waiting. When she had the heifer away from the other cattle, she pulled it to a trot so her father could catch the heifer's hind feet. That accomplished, they stretched her out on the ground.

The red Hereford's tongue hung from the side of her mouth as she struggled, her eyes wide with fear. Charity dismounted her palomino, the horse keeping the rope stretched taut, and met her father at the cow's side.

"Let's get this done," Flood said, holding one of several two-foot-long willow switches he'd brought along.

Charity stroked the frightened animal a few times on the neck, then put a knee on the heifer's shoulder and gripped her head. Her gloved hands slipped off the cow's slimy nose. She took a second hold. "I've got her."

"All right. Here we go." Flood squatted down and stuck the willow into the back of her throat, careful not to cause any harm.

The frightened animal opened her mouth but shut it quickly.

Charity took a firmer grip, ready to hold her mouth open once she gave in. "Come on, girl, this won't hurt a bit."

Flood tried again, this time lying in the dirt belly-down so he could get a better view to the back of her mouth. He squinted through the dust and flies. Admiration for all that her pa was filled her.

Flood tossed the switch away and rolled back to his knees. Climbing to his feet, he dusted off his clothes. "Yeah, I saw something that looked suspicious." He gave a small tug on his rope and his horse took a step forward. With the slack, Flood released the heifer's hind hooves and she struggled to stand. Charity and Flood stood back.

"You want to take her back to the ranch and I'll check the animals at Three Forks?"

She looked at the heifer that, now with her feet free, ran the length of the heading rope as far away from them as she could get. Her horse pivoted, keeping a taut line. "That'll take you a long time doing it alone."

"I've done it before and I'm sure I'll have to do it again."

"Okay, then," she replied.

"I'll see you at supper." He gave her the smile she remembered from childhood. She enjoyed working with her father just as much as she'd enjoyed sitting on his lap when she was four years old.

She pointed at him. "Be careful!"

He laughed, looking so much like her brothers, it took her breath. "*You* be careful, Charity. I mean that, girl!"

Chapter Eleven

Wednesday morning found Brandon behind his desk in the sheriff's office, going through the daily journal. One page. Two events, four sentences. Someday he'd have a deputy who followed his orders.

Each evening, even if the town was peaceful and nothing of consequence had happened, Brandon made a few quick notes. It helped with timetables if he had to backtrack on some larger issue. Jack's two entries were the Klinkner explosion and the near riot in the saloon that had been sparked by Hayden's mail-order bride.

Brandon snapped the book closed.

That reminded him, later this morning he planned to ride over to the mill and speak with Norman and Ina. Friday, he'd head out to the Heart of the Mountains and talk with Charity, then Saturday was the barn party at Luke's. He couldn't make up his mind on how he thought Charity would react to his news. One moment, he believed she'd be excited for him and totally open to the idea of moving, and the next, he thought this could be the end. But that was only if he decided to take the job.

He sighed. He missed her. After spending so much time together in Rio Wells, without her parents watching their every move, he knew he couldn't live without her. In the hayloft, she'd given him a small taste of her passion and he'd liked it very much. He always knew she'd be a match for him. And it was finally happening. In one month. He could hardly wait.

Jack hurried through the door. "We got us a telegram."

Brandon stood and took the message from his deputy.

NEED YOUR HELP IN PINE GROVE STOP COME RIGHT AWAY STOP

It was from the sheriff of Pine Grove, an elderly lawman who should have retired years ago, and who depended on Brandon probably more than he should.

Brandon's stomach tightened. "I wonder what this is about."

"Never know with Huxley."

Brandon looked out the door, thinking, then walked to the hat rack. "Looks like we'll be heading over to Pine Grove. I'll do a few errands and meet you back here in an hour."

"Shouldn't I stay in Y Knot?"

"No. It sounds urgent. If it is, and I need you, I don't want to have to wait for you to get there."

Jack didn't look all that pleased. Brandon could tell he was searching for an excuse to stay. "I'll let Hayden know he'll be in charge while we're gone. See if he'll stay in town."

"Fine," Jack bit out crossly. "Don't see why I just don't stay behind."

"Because Y Knot is paying you to work, not sit around. You got that?"

His face colored. "You bet, Brandon."

"I hope so."

Brandon rode down Creek Street, troubled by the news from Pine Grove. Dismounting at the hitching rail at the mill, he crossed over to the house as Ina opened the door and stepped out. She smiled.

"Thought that was you, Sheriff."

"Good morning, Ina," he replied, touching the brim of his hat. "Are Norman and Hayden around?"

"You'll find them hard at work in the mill—or at least you should."

Hayden spotted him as soon as he crossed the threshold of the tall planked building that smelled of freshly cut shavings and hot grease. He dropped the lever that released the belt. The circular blade slowed to a stop and quiet filled the area.

Norman looked up from where he'd been feeding the logs, and Morgan, the man Brandon had met last night at June's barn, came in from the back door. All three, dressed in their overalls and bandannas, ambled over to where he waited.

Hayden stuck out his hand and Brandon gripped it. "Heard you were back." Hayden's smile reached all the way to his eyes. He looked good. Well fed. Rested. Seemed married life agreed with him. "Glad you came out."

"Thanks, Hayden. Norman," he said with a nod. "Mr. Stanford."

Hayden chuckled. "Morgan mentioned meeting you in the livery. I'm sure he doesn't mind you calling him Morgan."

Morgan nodded but didn't say anything.

Norman, the shortest of the tall men, looked around at the faces. "Anything special bring you out, or is this a social call?"

"Up until about ten minutes ago it was going to be social, but now it's business. Hayden, can you stay in Y Knot a day or two and keep watch? You can call on the McCutcheons if the need arises."

"Sure. But why?"

Brandon pulled out the telegram and gave it to Hayden. Hayden read it aloud, then shook his head. "What's it about?"

"It's a mystery. But I'd rather be safe than sorry. I'm taking Jack with me."

"There's not much pressing here that Pa and Morgan can't manage," Hayden said. "Do you want me to come along to Pine Grove?"

"I'd feel better if you stayed in Y Knot. I'm not expecting to, but there's a possibility we might remain overnight."

Hayden smiled and clapped Morgan on the shoulder. "Do you mind me cutting out on the two of you?" he asked, looking between his brother-in-law and his father.

"'Course not," Morgan replied.

Hayden's smile widened. "I'll bring Heather along. I'm sure she'll like staying a night in the hotel."

Brandon couldn't fault his friend for wanting to show his girl a good time. "She won't distract you?"

"Yes, she will—that's the point. Not much happens in Y Knot, Brandon, don't worry."

"Thanks."

Brandon reached in his pocket and handed Hayden a silver badge.

Hayden was right. Seemed Brandon had missed the only excitement in years when he'd left after Charity. Being the sheriff in Y Knot meant acting as a go-between for shop owners with a burr under their saddle, housing drunks on the weekend so they could sleep off a snoot full, and lining up the townsfolk who had complaints to air when Judge Wesley came through. His last big case was three years ago when he arrested Earl Morton and Will Dixon, the men who'd hamstrung the McCutcheons' yearling bull.

"I'd best be going," he said. "I still have a few things to do." Like get a note to Charity telling her he'd come out to the ranch tomorrow evening. Most likely, she'd have Esperanza cook up some nice meal.

A bout of nerves tightened his stomach when he tried to envision how the touchy conversation would go. He'd tell her about the upcoming interview with Timberlake, and how much this opportunity meant to him. Then, if she was receptive, he'd ask her thoughts on the possibility of moving to Kansas City after they married—if he got the job.

Those were a lot of ifs.

"Do you have time to come in the house and meet Heather?" Hayden asked. "She's been listening to all our stories about you and Charity."

And surely getting a good laugh. "Any other time I would," Brandon said honestly. He truly was curious about the woman who had tamed his friend so quickly. "I have a few things to accomplish before we head over to Pine Grove. How about I meet her at Luke's shindig this Saturday night? We're announcing our engagement there."

Brandon laughed to chase away the pinch of worry in his gut. *We will be announcing it, won't we?*

"Funny to have a party for a one-month engagement." He shrugged. "But then I don't know the ways of women and what goes through their minds."

Norman shook a finger in his face. "Pay attention. Those things are important to the fairer sex, son. The sooner you learn that, the happier you'll be."

A silly smile curved Hayden's lips. "Same thing he told me. And you know, it's true."

"I'm off, then." Brandon turned on his heel and went for his horse, the troubling telegram still in his hand. He'd head home, throw a few things in his saddlebag, and meet Jack back at the office. Before that, he'd stop by the Hitching Post to see if the mop boy would ride out to the McCutcheons' with his message. The kid had done it before in the past for two bits. With any luck, he'd be free to do it again today.

Chapter Twelve

Charity rode into the ranch yard, the heifer still straggling at the end of her rope. Frustrated as all get-out from tussling with the young heifer every step of the way, she slumped in the saddle while she wet her bandanna with water from her canteen. She swabbed her face, enjoying the cool, wet rag on her sun-scorched skin. It had been a hot two-hour ride home. The whole day, the sky had been cloudless, giving the sun full rein.

The bunkhouse porch was deserted, the ranch house quiet. She spotted two new steers in the sick corral, put there by one of the other cowhands. Hers would make five. As soon as she accomplished the chore of depositing the stubborn animal into the pen without letting the others escape, she'd go inside and take a nice cool bath.

Her heifer mooed pitifully to the others, and they looked her way. Charity dallied up short, with the intention of dragging the young cow inside, when the sound of buggy wheels drew her attention to the road that led from town to the ranch. She squinted.

After a second look, she recognized the driver as the young man who offered his mop and bucket around town to any business that would pay. She'd seen him a few times dumping water off the boardwalk in front of the saloon, or inside one of the shops. Next to him sat a beautiful woman.

Charity wiped her arm across her damp, gritty face, knowing she must look like hell.

The buggy drew to a halt a few feet away. The woman, of unspeakable beauty, wore a dress much too elaborate for a rancher's wife. Her hair was coifed just so, and her piercing blue eyes didn't miss a thing.

Charity shifted in the saddle uncomfortably. Before she could ask what they wanted, Roady and Matt galloped into the yard, dismounted at the bunkhouse hitching rail, then beat a path over to the buggy as if their pants were on fire.

"How do, Fancy. Harold," Roady said, tipping his hat.

Fancy!

Matthew greeted them, then glanced at Charity and nodded. His amused expression at her dusty, disheveled appearance was irritating.

"Hello, boys," Fancy purred. She glanced at Charity as if waiting to be introduced.

With his hat in his hands, Matthew jumped at the chance. "This is my little sister, Charity. Charity, this is Fancy Aubrey, the new saloon girl at the Hitching Post. She arrived in Y Knot when you were out of town."

Of course she's Fancy Aubrey. I should have known at first glance!

Charity didn't know what to think of her brother and Roady acting like fools over the saloon woman who hadn't been a *girl* for a good fifteen years, if Charity were to guess.

"I'm pleased to make your acquaintance, *Miss* Aubrey," she said, pasting on a confident smile. "What brings you out our way this warm afternoon?" She was tempted to add, *Brandon's not here.*

Before the woman could answer, Roady propped his boot on the step board on Fancy's side of the buggy and leaned forward. "We were surprised as all get-out to see your buggy pull onto the property."

"It's still a free country, Mr. Guthrie, the last time I checked." Her eyes flashed a challenge and her chin tipped up.

"You misunderstood," Matt said quickly. "It's just that not many visitors come calling way out here."

"Actually, I have a note for Miss Charity," Harold said, holding out a twice-folded piece of paper. "From the sheriff."

Without invitation, Fancy took the note from Harold's hand and leaned out of the buggy, handing it up to Charity when she rode forward. Their eyes met.

"Harold had just agreed to take me for a buggy ride when Brandon—" She broke off, then amended with a beautiful smile, "When Sheriff Crawford came into the saloon." A slight blush colored her cheeks, but Charity didn't miss the shrewd look in her eyes.

A double dose of jealousy hit her like a locomotive breaking from its track. Thoughts of Brandon drooling over the curvaceous beauty had her warmer under her collar than she already was from ranching in the hot sun. It didn't help that Matt and Roady were acting like schoolboys.

"Thank you, Harold. I appreciate you coming all the way out here."

Fancy waved her handkerchief and then touched it to her nose as if something—possibly Charity's filthy clothes—wasn't quite to her liking. "We best let you get back to whatever it was you were doing."

From her dressing table, with a towel still wrapped around her wet hair, Charity glanced at the note from Brandon on her bed, still folded exactly where she'd tossed it. It might be childish of her, but she'd yet to read it. Just something about it coming from *that* woman set her teeth on edge.

She'd concocted a vision of the sexy woman and Brandon talking and laughing. It played over and over in her mind without respite, no matter how hard she tried to divert her thoughts. Exactly like what Francis told her at the bunkhouse.

Had Brandon used the excuse of sending her a message as a legitimate way of seeking out Fancy Aubrey?

Obviously, the two had talked about her. It didn't feel right. Even if the bath had done wonders to ease away her tense muscles from so many hours in the saddle, her mind was still uneasy. *But it's not Brandon's fault that Harold already had a chore to do*, she argued with herself. He hadn't known Harold had agreed to take Fancy for a ride this afternoon.

Charity didn't like the bitter feel of insecurity wedged in the pit of her stomach. She wasn't usually the jealous type—at least since the trip to Texas. It was generally the other way around.

She unwrapped the towel from her hair and worked her comb through her strawberry-blond locks, detangling as she went. Unable to withstand her curiosity any longer, she went over to her bed. So what if Fancy Aubrey had read Brandon's personal correspondence to her? It wasn't in an envelope, so that possibility was likely. There wasn't one thing she could do to change what had already transpired, so she'd just have to accept it or go crazy.

The sight of Brandon's bold print brought a flush of warmth to her insides. Smiling, she pictured his hand holding his pencil—writing a love letter to *her*, not Fancy Aubrey or any other woman. She was a lucky girl—and she'd best remember that.

My dearest Charity,
The days since our parting have been the longest of my life.

He *was* missing her, just as her mother had predicted. The month-long wait had him dreaming and writing letters.

You've made me a happy man by agreeing to become my wife. The days can't pass fast enough to suit me. I should have thought a bit longer when your mother suggested we wait. I'd like to come out to the ranch to see you tomorrow evening. I have things to discuss before the barn party the following night. I can't wait to kiss you...

Your devoted husband-to-be,
Brandon

Postscript—I am going to Pine Grove to look into some matter Sheriff Huxley telegrammed me about.

Charity reached up and touched her lips. She thought of the kiss they'd shared when he'd saved her from the rattlesnake in Rio Wells, and again later in the hayloft right above Uncle Winston.

She shivered, then closed her eyes, imagining what being his wife would be like.

"I have things to discuss before the barn party the following night."

What did he mean? What could he want to talk about? Putting an end to this wait to get married? She sighed happily. She'd wholeheartedly agree if that was on his mind. He was an exceptional man.

Charity Crawford…she liked the sound of that. Now, she needed to stop daydreaming and remember to ask her mother about dinner, and what they should prepare to dazzle Brandon.

After a hard, fast ride, Brandon and Jack reined up at the sheriff's office in Pine Grove. It didn't take a moment for the sheriff and his pot-bellied deputy, Archie Bly, to meet them in the street.

"Over here," the sheriff said, calling Brandon and the others to follow.

They crossed the road to the undertaker's. A calf was stretched out next to the bodies of two men on a tabletop expansive enough to hold five or six corpses. Old Man Pickens, the undertaker, looked none too happy about having a bovine in his establishment. The pungent air hung dank in the room as the men gathered around. Death had a life of its own.

"You brought a *dead calf* inside?" Brandon couldn't disguise his incredulity.

Sheriff Huxley tipped his head. "Didn't want to feed the evidence to the wolves. Besides, saves my back from bending over."

To each his own. "So, what happened?" Brandon gestured to the dead men on the table, both somewhere in their late twenties. Clean shaven; store-bought clothes. One had a hand-tooled belt that looked like it cost a pretty penny, with the letters DG carved in the tip. The younger of the two's face was contorted in a grimace, as if he'd seen something horrible just before he died. Each had a single gunshot wound to the chest. "You know 'em?"

"This one." The sheriff pointed to the victim on the left. "Drake Greenly. Lived an hour's ride out of town by the river and come in once or twice a month for supplies. Had a claim out there. I don't know the other. Owner of the mercantile said they was in last week, and thought he remembered Greenly calling him Smith. They was arguing and cussing each other out every other sentence. He heard Drake mumbling about giving Smith his due."

Brandon nodded. He fingered through the contents that had been taken from Greenly's pockets. A small knife, a nail, and three pennies.

"Where'd you find 'em? Any horses around? Or signs of a struggle? Looks like this happened yesterday or the day before."

"Speak up, Crawford," Huxley barked. "You know I'm going deaf." Deep grooves marked the old man's face and hands.

Brandon wondered if the grumpy codger was still up to the job. He repeated his questions.

"I didn't call you here for the men. It's obvious they killed each other in a pistol duel. Only worry now is who'll pay the undertaker to bury 'em since they only had three pennies to their names." He shook his head in disgust. "Damn hotheads. It's the calf. See here." He pointed to the animal's shoulder, and then his hip.

The calf! "You telegrammed me about a dead steer?"

"Killing stock is breaking the law, same as robbing the bank." Huxley glanced at all the men in succession, as if looking for affirmation. "Maybe someone just wanted a quick supper and got scared off before he could finish the job, since the little critter's still intact. Strange, though, he was killed by arrows—two of 'em, not bullets. But the bad shots are curious to me."

He pointed again to the back, and then the hip. "Either we got us an Indian with bad eyesight, or we got a cagey poacher wanting us to think we have an Indian with bad eyesight. Either way, I want 'em caught. Brandon, since you're a darn good tracker, thought you could help me find the culprit. Ranchers don't take kindly to anyone killing their stock—and neither do I. Any of my citizens found breaking the law in this town will pay the fine."

"You summoned me to track a poacher?" Brandon couldn't keep the irritation from his voice. "What about your deputy?" he said, looking at the man standing next to Jack.

"Archie ain't worth squat."

Jack smirked and Archie sputtered angrily.

"I'd do it myself, but you know my eyesight ain't what it used to be." The old lawman swiped a hand across his mouth. "Besides, didn't I just say you're the best tracker in the territory?"

Holding his temper, Brandon stared into the man's face until he felt his anger fizzle out. He'd grow old someday too. Resigned, he bent over the calf, looking at the wounds. "You been out where he was found?"

"Not yet. I was waiting on you."

"How'd he get here?"

"Rancher brought him in."

Brandon didn't mind Sheriff Huxley calling on him for important matters. He was happy to assist, if he could. It was just he felt a sharp tug of urgency to get back to Y Knot. If he could only talk Charity into getting married directly and going with him to Kansas City. They'd turn the trip into a honeymoon. The more he thought about it, the more he felt he could convince her—and she'd see it as a sign of how much she meant to him. He rubbed his palms together in anticipation. That would work just fine.

"Brandon?" The sheriff was waiting on his reply.

He nodded. "Let's go see what we can find. Jack, you may as well head back to town and relieve Hayden."

"Will do," Jack said, clearly pleased to get out of the work ahead. "When d' you think you'll be back?"

"This shouldn't take me long. Most likely tonight or tomorrow morning."

Outside, he drew in a lungful of clean, fresh air. He'd get the mystery about the calf cleared up and get his tail back to Y Knot and the ranch.

Chapter Thirteen

Friday morning dawned to overcast skies. Charity looked out her window, missing Brandon with all her heart. The chickens in the yard faced into the wind, their feathers ruffled as they pecked at the dirt. Lucky meandered out onto the bunkhouse porch, taking his hourly gauge of the weather that approached from the west.

When she heard excited voices coming from below, Charity hurried across her bedroom and out onto the upstairs landing.

Amy came through the door with Cinder in her arms. Faith, with Dawn and Holly, was already in the room speaking with her mother, along with Rachel carrying little Beth—a shortening of her middle name, Elizabeth, because Rachel and Matt had named her after Faith when Luke's wife all but saved the child during her difficult birth. That was a day Charity would never forget!

No boys in sight. It was a rare occasion to keep them in the house with their younger female cousins for long. They preferred to be out ranching with the men. Riding and roping and getting dirty.

"Good morning," Charity called down happily, noticing Rachel's and Amy's protruding bellies. The women looked up and waved, a little windblown but beautiful. Their expanding waistlines looked so cute.

"Mornin'!" Dawn all but shouted in an excited three-year-old's voice. She dashed for the stairs faster than any toddler should be able to run, and climbed with the same swiftness, her cousin Beth trailing in her footsteps. Dawn vaulted into Charity's embrace with the force of a runaway calf, almost knocking her down.

"Whoa, little one, you're strong," Charity yelped after catching her balance. She swung Dawn around with a laugh. Putting her down quickly, she got ready for Beth's assault.

"That comes from having an older brother and a father who like to roughhouse all the time," Faith said. "I keep telling Luke he's creating a handful, and he'll be sorry when she runs off all her suitors with her strength and sense of competition."

Charity now had Beth in full swing. The child's brown calico dress swished out like a bell. Dawn waited with upstretched hands for another turn.

Rachel watched with a smile as she rubbed the bulge at her waist. "We came to talk about the party tomorrow, and about the wedding. We need to set the wheels in motion."

A bit winded, Charity took each niece by the hand, marveling at how different the two girls were, and yet how the same. Where Dawn was fair, with blue eyes and hair like sunshine, accentuated by a splash of freckles across the top of her nose, Beth had Rachel's darker coloring and coffee-colored eyes. Both were adorable. As was Cinder, their two-year-old cousin, with straight black hair as shiny as polished obsidian. That child watched their descent from Amy's arms, a tiny smile curving her lips. When the three were back down among the group, Cinder clapped her hands together with flourish.

Amy dumped a cloth bag of toys out onto the middle of the rug in front of the large living room window. There were several dolls with soft hair made from red yarn, an old cigar box, more than a few blocks, and two toy chickens carved of wood.

Dawn and Beth pulled away from Charity and raced to get to the rag dolls first. Cinder reached her arms out with a cry, so Amy set her feet on the ground and she toddled over. Rachel pointed to a satchel by the door. "When they grow tired of those, I also brought along some things to occupy little hands."

"Wonderful," Claire said. "You girls get comfortable and I'll go see what's keeping Esperanza with the tea. Have you all eaten?"

Nods went around the room.

"Good. We have work to do that shouldn't be put off another day. A month will be gone before we know it." Her mother looked over to her. "Charity, entertain the girls until I get back."

Claire swished across the floor in her full-length skirt and disappeared into the kitchen.

Amy sat down first and patted the cushion. "Sit here, Charity. I've hardly had a chance to chat with you since you got back."

Charity complied, and Faith sat next to her. Rachel took the chair across from the sofa.

Claire returned and got comfortable. "What should we talk about first?"

"I want to hear about Brandon and how he proposed," Faith said. She jiggled Holly in her arms when the baby opened her eyes and started to fuss. "You never did say."

Everyone's attention was riveted on her. "I, well—" She felt her face warming up.

Rachel laughed. "That's all right. Some things aren't meant to share. When will we see him next? At the party?"

Charity heaved a sigh of relief and thanked Rachel with her eyes. "No. Actually, he's coming out this evening for dinner, just the four of us. He sent word by way of Y Knot's mop boy." *I won't give the saloon girl a mention.* "Every moment without him feels like an hour."

Rachel leaned in, a smile on her face.

"Now he's sending love letters?" Faith teased. She glanced around at all the women's faces. "Quite romantic. He's changed a lot in the last few months. Hasn't he, Charity?"

That was an understatement. It felt like a whirlwind since she'd left for Texas under the pretense of attending finishing school. "He has—and then sometimes I think he hasn't changed a bit."

Her mother cleared her throat. "Time is running short and we must stay on track. What do you think about the wedding cake? Charity likes spice—as do I—but Brandon prefers chocolate…"

Brandon took off his hat and wiped his forehead with the sleeve of his shirt, praying the rain would hold off for a few hours longer.

"Brandon?"

At the sound of Huxley's voice, he secured his hat back on his head and walked to where the horses were tied.

"Find anything new?" Pine Grove's sheriff asked.

"Nothing. But that doesn't mean it's not here." He scanned the far hillside, perplexed. "Someone went to a heck of a lot of trouble covering their trail." He'd circled the area more times than he could count. "Only thing I see are the tracks left by the rancher who brought the calf in."

The sheriff gathered his reins. "I say we head back and return in the morning."

Brandon looked around, agitated. He didn't like admitting defeat. The perpetrator couldn't just disappear into thin air—unless it *was* an Indian. They were much harder to track than whites.

"Aren't you coming?" The expression on Huxley's face was one of disbelief when Brandon squatted and ran his hand over the golden-brown grass one more time. "What're you gonna do out here? Ain't nothing more to learn. Besides, looks like rain."

"That's just it. If there is evidence to find, I need to do it now, before the rain washes it away. I'm not ready to give up quite yet."

Chapter Fourteen

Ike tucked his fiddle under his chin and drew the bow across the strings skillfully for such a grizzled old cowhand. The notes weaved through the air like magic, the sound a silky ribbon fluttering in the breeze. The melody moved Charity's heart.

Lucky and Smokey joined in with their guitars, creating a beautiful sonata. Several nicely dressed couples swung out into the middle of the barn to waltz. The straw on the ground provided a nice, shuffle-inducing dance floor.

Charity took note when her parents followed suit, moving together as perfectly as if they were made for each other. Her mother gazed up into her pa's eyes, unmindful of who might be watching them.

Charity tried to smile as she tapped her foot with the music, but the corners of her mouth wobbled. After Brandon hadn't shown up last night for dinner, she'd asked Roady to ride into town to see if he was all right. Roady returned with the news that Brandon was still in Pine Grove. Jack Jones was back and said the issue was nothing much, just a case of butchered stock, and that Brandon intended to be at the party tonight.

Jack had arrived alone an hour ago—and now stood with a cup of punch by the open double doors with Mr. Lichtenstein and Mr. Simpson, the merchant's forgetful clerk. He'd come with no news about Brandon.

Luke meandered his way through the crowd toward where she was more or less hiding in the shadows by the empty stalls.

"What're you doing back here in the dark?" he asked. "I've been looking for you for ten minutes. Everyone wants to talk to you. Congratulate you."

"I don't feel much like socializing without Brandon," she replied sullenly. "What if something's happened to him? What if he's hurt and needs help?" She'd wanted to send out a search party after what Roady had reported last night, but Luke and the rest absolutely forbade it.

"Nothing's happened to Brandon. He'll be here. He won't mess this up." He tipped her chin up with a gentle finger. "You better get used to him getting called away. He takes his job seriously, and that's what makes him a darn good lawman. You're made of stronger stuff, Charity McCutcheon. There's a party going on and you're the guest of honor. Do you want to make all the guests feel bad?"

Luke's tone brooked no argument—and he was right. Just because she was down didn't mean she should ruin the night for everyone else. She squared her shoulders, pasted on a smile, and pushed away her doubt about Brandon. She'd taken her mother's words seriously her first night home, but maybe there was something to her intuitions. Maybe Brandon *had* been having second thoughts about marrying her and just didn't know how to break it to her. Perhaps his absence last night, and now tonight, was his way of letting her down easy without having to explain himself. A flash of anger zipped through her before she reminded herself he'd just sent her that nice note. Brandon would never abandon her. Not after everything they'd been through together.

Luke grasped her hand and dragged her out to the middle of the dance floor, mixing into the flow of dancers next to Chance and Evie, and Matt and Rachel. Everyone in the room clapped when they saw her.

"There you are," Rachel said. "I've been looking for you."

Hayden caught her eye from the punch bowl area and waved. Charity had yet to meet his wife, Heather, who stood next to him and another tall, dark-haired man who was unfamiliar to Charity. June Pittman was here too. Seemed the whole town had turned out.

On the next revolution, Charity answered, "I've been over there." She pointed to the back of the barn.

Rachel gasped. "That's no place for you! You can still have fun until Brandon shows up. Any word yet?"

She shook her head. It was almost seven o'clock. The side of beef cooking over the fire pit would soon be sliced up and the rest of the dinner brought out to the table. The night would be gone before Brandon made a showing. Not to mention, she had spent two hours dressing. She couldn't smell any sweeter if she tried.

The music stopped and the musicians put their instruments down. It was the first break in an hour, and the silence at once sounded deafening.

Chance and Evie smiled. "Good to see you dancing, Charity," Chance said. "No need to worry over Brandon. He can take care of himself. But while you're waiting, I'd like to introduce you to a newcomer to town who arrived when you were gone."

A lot of that happening lately. She thanked Luke for the dance, then followed Chance and Evie to the barn doors, feeling like a third wheel without Brandon. She smiled and nodded at friends. Chance stopped next to a new fellow standing by himself, who, even though he tried to cover it, looked bored. His sandy blond hair, cut just below his ears, was neatly combed, and his shirt was pressed. "This is Tobit Preece," Chance said. "He's relatively new to Y Knot. He lives several miles past our place with his grandfather. Tobit, this is Charity McCutcheon."

A surge of memories made her smile. As a girl, she'd galloped Buttercup, her first horse, over the meadows that bordered the Preece farm, splashing through the river on especially hot days. "Your grandfather is Isaiah Preece?"

"That's correct, miss," he said with a somewhat shy smile.

Charity couldn't stop her smile from widening. "How is he? I haven't seen him in a very long time."

"He gets around fair t'middling for a man who will be eighty-five this year. Well enough to drive the buckboard to town once a day, delivering milk to the mercantile, and to check on things 'round the farm I'm supposed to get done."

Tobit had a slight Southern accent, which made all his words sound warm and inviting.

"I'm happy to hear that. When I was just a girl, I used to ride my horse up the river and venture out your way. I used to think him the nicest man in the world. If he spotted me, he was always so friendly. And he'd talk up a storm."

His mouth quirked. "That sounds like Gramps. Never lets his chores interfere with his jawing."

She looked around. "Is he here tonight?"

"No, he stayed home."

Charity liked Tobit's eyes. They were kind and inquisitive. Showed an intelligent wisdom. "I have to say, I'm surprised to meet you. I wasn't aware Isaiah had any children, let alone a grandson. He never said anything."

Tobit's smile dimmed.

Me and my big mouth. The moment the words were out, she wished she could call them back.

"Tobit has a lot of new plans for the farm," Evie said, skillfully changing the subject. "And he's sketched it all out on a big board, so even a city girl like me can understand."

Thank God for Evie. "That sounds really nice, Tobit."

"Charity," Faith called, waving from across the barn. "Can you come here?"

She nodded, and snagged Tobit's gaze. "Be sure to tell your grandfather Charity McCutcheon says hello, and that I'm going to come out to see him sometime soon. Also, that I'm delighted to meet his grandson." She reached out and touched his arm. "All the McCutcheons are, Tobit. Now that you know us, don't be a stranger."

Tobit shook his head, then smiled at the Holcombs. "No, miss. Chance and Evie have taken me under their wing and are working hard to make sure I meet absolutely everyone in Y Knot."

Feeling a bit better, Charity set her hands on her hips. "And to think I thought I was special." They all laughed.

Brandon rode toward Luke and Faith's barn, which was full to overflowing with townsfolk. Buggies and wagons were everywhere. Horses were tied to hitching posts and trees. The sounds of laughter and the buzz of friends talking drifted out through the darkness to meet him.

He glanced around, miffed at being kept away for so long. After completing several more chores for the good sheriff of Pine Grove that had taken a full day and a half, he'd gone back out one more time to examine the area where the calf had been found. After widening his search, he'd found a new set of horse tracks. Then two more. After climbing a steep embankment, one horse had headed toward Y Knot and the Heart of the Mountains, and then up to Luke's.

He didn't know if it had anything to do with the dead calf, or perhaps with the men Huxley felt sure had killed each other, but it was disturbing that the trail led here. At this point, nothing about the Pine Grove case made much sense. He *did* know he was trail weary. His travel plans still needed to be worked out. He'd stood Charity up last night. And now he was arriving late to his own party.

A shout went up from the partygoers when he was still fifty feet away.

Everyone turned. They waved and called to him, their voices exuberant and cheerful in the cool evening air. It wasn't but a moment before Charity spotted him.

In a flurry of fabric, she dashed in his direction, holding up the front of her pretty dress so she wouldn't trip. Her hair bounced on her shoulders, her eyes wide with excitement and relief.

He could tell she'd gone to great lengths preparing for this night, which made his own trail-worn appearance seem all the worse. The letter from Kansas City pricked his mind.

He wished he could just forget about the job interview, the letter, and what it represented. Pretend he'd never received it—surely, he did. If he had returned from Texas a week later, it would have been out of his hands. But he knew he wouldn't.

Timberlake. His parents' death. After all these years. A connection more real than his dreams.

As Charity ran toward him, he wondered: Was this a great opportunity, or the biggest mistake of his life?

Chapter Fifteen

Brandon dismounted and dropped his reins in time to swoop Charity into a massive hug. He kissed her lips, not caring who might see.

"I'm so sorry, darlin'. I wanted to be here sooner—to be here last night."

"Oh, Brandon! I thought something had happened to you. That you were shot or killed."

Her words against his mouth were sweet until he tasted her tears.

"Or that you were hurt somewhere and there wasn't anyone to help you. That I'd never see you again."

He took her face between his palms. With his thumbs, he wiped away her tears, then kissed each eye. "I'm sorry. I hate that I worried you. But it couldn't be helped. I got caught up with this issue in Pine Grove. Can you ever forgive me?"

She wrapped her arms around his middle and laid her head against his chest. "Now I can. Now that you're here and alive—and nothing more can go wrong."

"I must smell like a horse." He tried to take a step back, but she squeezed him tighter.

"You're not going anywhere, Sheriff, so just get that thought out of your head this instant," she said against his chest, her spunk returning. "You owe me a thousand dances, a thousand hugs, and a thousand kisses."

He chuckled. "All tonight?"

"Yep."

"Well, we better get moving, then. I see some brothers of yours on their way out here."

Charity groaned. She eased up enough to look over her shoulder. "Can't they *ever* leave us be?"

"I don't think so. It's their job to look after you."

"Soon that job will belong solely to you," Charity said. "And I can't wait."

He turned her away from inquisitive eyes for one more quick kiss. "I'm counting the minutes for that job, but you may be mistaken about your brothers relinquishing their hold on you. They won't be giving that up anytime soon."

"Brandon," Matt said when he arrived at their side with Luke and Mark. His brow arched at the sight of his little sister and the firm hold she had on Brandon's hand. "Jack filled us in on the situation in Pine Grove. Did you find out anything more?"

"Not much." He pulled Charity close and sent them a meaningful look. He'd not spoil another evening for her. Later, when he was alone with the men, he'd tell them he'd finally spotted a trail to follow. And surprisingly, it had led to their ranch, and now to Luke's. He'd keep a sharp eye out tonight for anything that looked suspicious. Besides, with so many men here, the guests were safe if those responsible intended anything other than a good time.

Matt slapped his shoulder. "Tomorrow's another day. Maybe you'll have more luck then. Let's get back to the party. Flood should be finished slicing the beef. Hope you're hungry."

Brandon barked out a laugh. "Hungry? Look at me." He gestured to the two-day growth of whiskers that covered his jaw. "I'm not only starving, I need a good soak and shave."

"You look handsome to me," Charity said, walking next to his side. She'd yet to release his hand. "I like this rugged look." She looked up at him with stars in her eyes, and he reminded himself just how fortunate he was.

"You like anything he does," Mark said. "I remember the time he made you jealous by talking with Lynn Dray at Mr. Lichtenstein's ice cream social. You didn't think he was so wonderful then."

Charity laughed. "He wasn't talking, he was *flirting*—outrageously. I remember that night well. You can't blame me for dumping that bowl of ice cream over his head. I was only a girl. And it felt really good. That doesn't count."

Mark gave his sister a pointed look. "You were thirteen. Plenty old enough to act like a lady, if you'd been so inclined. Mother was scandalized, as were we all. Even weeks later, the cowhands turned pink when anyone broached the subject."

Brandon rubbed the top of his head with one hand, and carried his hat, along with the reins of his bridle, in the other. "Don't be hard on her, boys, I liked it. Cooled me off right quick and made my hair shiny for a week. As I recall, I actually enjoyed it when it started to melt and run down my face. Besides, it told me that Charity cared a lot more than she was letting on. I had to do something to get her attention."

Charity gasped. "You rascal! I couldn't get your goat no matter how hard I tried. I went home and cried for a week."

He pulled her to a stop. "I never knew that," he said regretfully. "You cried for a week?" The thought of her miserable over him hurt. He never wanted to be a source of pain to her again.

"I cried more than that over you. I cried all the time. I just never let you know."

"Holy smokes," Luke complained. "This is getting deep."

"By the way, Sheriff," Charity said, her chin tilting to the side, a sure sign trouble was on the way. "Just how well do you know Fancy Aubrey anyway—and *why* is she on a first-name basis with *you*?"

Her brothers burst into laughter, giving him the opportunity to swing Charity around in his arms and kiss her. "Not near as well as I know *you*, missy! You've got nothing to worry about."

Back with the crowd, everyone gathered around and offered Brandon and Charity their good wishes for the upcoming event. Dr. Handerhoosen gave his congratulations, as did old Mr. Herrick, owner of the leather shop. All the while, Brandon paid close attention to the guests, taking note of who was where, and made sure everyone was accounted for.

Stories flowed for a good twenty minutes until Flood called them over to get their plates. "Come and get it. The best beef you'll get *any* side of the Rockies."

"Enjoy that status while you can, Mr. McCutcheon," Chance joked. "Come next year, I'm going to have that claim."

"With what?" Luke threw out, a big grin on his face. "Those fancy-pants French steers?"

"You bet your life. They're maturing right nice. You wait and see."

Brandon watched Chance's new wife nod with pride and then rub his arm affectionately. They made a nice couple. And soon, there'd be a little Chance running around. Imagine that. Pretty hard to believe, considering.

Brandon warmed at the thought of having a son to hold, teach to ride, take fishing. He'd give that little man all the time he'd lost with his father—and then some. He was tired of being alone. He was ready to make a life with Charity and create a family to call his own.

After dinner and desserts of apple-gingerbread cobbler and sweet potato pie, followed by another hour of dancing, the party began to wind down. Several families gathered up their belongings and children and departed in groups. Ike, Lucky, and Smokey packed up their instruments and headed for the bunkhouse, all smiles after the night of waltzes and merrymaking. Roady lounged against the barn door opening and watched him and Charity take one more round on the dance floor to imaginary music. The women had gone inside to bundle up the sleepy children for the ride home.

Charity's face rested in the crook of his neck. As he marveled at how good she felt in his arms, Roady pushed away from the wall and cocked his head. Listening to something. He went to the loft ladder and climbed up. Brandon didn't think anything of it until Roady yelled down for some help.

"Charity, go fetch the others from the house," Brandon said as he headed to the ladder, gun drawn from his holster and ready. "Roady," he called halfway up. "What's wrong?"

"Just get up here. I need your help."

At the top, Brandon hoisted himself onto the landing, expecting the worst.

"I thought I heard something, so I came to investigate." Roady squatted next to an Indian girl who was stretched out in the hay. He lifted her wrist, feeling for a pulse. "She's barely alive. This wound in her shoulder looks several days old."

Brandon holstered his gun. The girl was smaller than Charity and must be several years younger. Her buckskin breeches clung to her slim shape, and the talisman that hung off the side of her chest signaled she was a warrior. She had a large knife sheath tied around her waist with buckskin straps.

Roady looked around the dark interior. "Let's get her down." He gathered her in his arms.

Brandon heard the pounding of boots and men's voices as they responded to Charity's summons. The loft vibrated when someone grasped the ladder. Brandon called out, "Hold up. We're bringing her down."

"Her?" It was Luke's voice.

"Yeah. She's unconscious. Someone go catch the doctor before he gets too far down the road."

Roady brought the girl over to the edge of the loft.

Brandon descended a few rungs and Roady placed her in his arms. The men below steadied him as he descended. Who was this young woman? Where had she come from? And most important, why?

Brandon hoped she would survive to provide the answers.

Chapter Sixteen

Luke reached up and steadied Brandon as he came slowly down the rungs. Flood and Matt leaned in, offering their help. Luke blinked, not trusting his vision in the dim interior of the barn. Supple buckskin, with fringe running up the sides, encased the girl's legs, and her silky jet-black hair hung over Brandon's arms like a blanket. The girl he held was not a neighbor from the party, like he'd been expecting.

Charity gasped. "An Indian girl?" Her gaze sought Luke's, drawn, he was sure, by his half-breed status. She blinked, then looked away, almost guilty at being caught. "What's she doing in the barn?"

The question went unanswered. Roady came down a few rungs of the ladder behind Brandon, then jumped the rest of the way. Without a pause, he put out his hands, as if by being the one to find her, he'd staked his claim. Brandon shifted her limp body over to him. The cowhand gathered her wounded arm close to her body and laid it over her abdomen.

"Not just any Indian woman," Brandon said. "A warrior."

"Girl," Luke corrected.

"That may be," Brandon went on, standing eye to eye with him. "But I've heard they can be just as fierce as any male warrior—maybe even more so because they have more to prove."

"What on earth?" Claire stepped forward.

Luke glanced over to see how his mother would take this unusual turn of events. Regret surged up in his throat, remembering her history of being abducted by Indians when she was a young woman, then living in the Indian camp for almost a year. He couldn't imagine what she was feeling.

"Brandon, you think this could be the person you've been tracking?" Luke asked. An unusual sensation snaked down his spine, as if all their lives would never be quite the same after this night.

"Most likely."

Fingers lingering on the soft buckskin shirt, Charity jerked her face up to Luke's and then over to Brandon's.

Faith and the other women slowly came forward.

"What do you mean, the person you've been tracking?" Charity asked angrily. "Brandon, why didn't you tell me what was going on as soon as you arrived?" She looked from face to face. "All of us, for that matter? We're not children."

"Charity's right," Claire said, now standing at her daughter's side. "It never astounds me how dense men can be when it comes to protecting their women. It's downright irritating." She laid a quivering hand on the girl's brow. "She's burning up. Let's get her inside."

Luke nodded and stood aside. "Take her up to the guest bedroom, Roady. Mark should be back with the doctor anytime now."

"I don't know if she'll make it through the night," Dr. Handerhoosen said once he'd examined her. "By the depth of her wound, she's probably lost an incredible amount of blood. And she's thin. I'm sure she hasn't had anything substantial to eat for some time."

Dark crimson swirled in the basin of water on the nightstand as he washed. He took the towel Faith offered him and dried his hands. After drawing the sheet over the girl's limp form, he took his stethoscope from around his neck and put it in his medical bag and snapped it closed.

Luke and the rest of the family crowded inside the bedroom, watching. Colton, Billy, and Adam, the oldest children, were still awake. They stood in the doorway, worried expressions stamped on their brows.

"What do we do for her?" Claire asked. Something about his mother's concern put Luke on edge. What was she thinking? She hadn't stopped hugging herself since Brandon had carried the Indian maid down from the loft, as though a deep chill had settled in her bones.

"All you can do is help her fight the infection by feeding her fortifying food when she's able to eat. I've cleaned and disinfected the wound." The doctor glanced at her gauze-wrapped arm. "I'll be out early tomorrow morning to check on her progress. It's bleeding pretty good again from my probing and washing. Removing the bark and dirt was vital. Otherwise, it wouldn't have healed until every wood particle festered out. By then, infection might have taken her arm, or her life." He gave them all a stern look. "Her chances are iffy, at best. If she'd been found yesterday, the outcome might have been different."

Charity stood on the opposite side of the bed, still holding Brandon's hand. "She'll wake up, doctor."

The stubborn tilt to her brows, which Luke knew all too well, said she believed it.

When Dr. Handerhoosen had gathered his things and left, Flood stepped away from the wall. "Amy, Rachel, go gather the children. I'll get the wagon ready to take you all home. I'm sure they'd like to wake up in their own beds."

When he slung his arm over Claire's shoulders, she gazed up at him. "I'd prefer to stay a while longer, Flood. Help Luke and Faith with the—" She shut her eyes for a moment, and when she opened them, she stared at the drawn face on the pillow before looking to her husband. "I'd just feel better. If I go home, I won't sleep a wink."

Flood straightened up to his full height. His mouth turned into a hard, flat line. "You're worn out, woman. First Charity, then this party. You'll get sick yourself if you don't take some rest."

Claire stepped out from under his arm and walked over to the end of the bed, as if making her stand. "I'm staying—for a while longer at least. I've made up my mind and you won't change it."

Her tone was hard. This might be the only time Luke had heard his mother refuse a request.

Luke found Faith's gaze, and her brows lifted. Rachel and Amy sought their husbands' comforting arms. Tense moments between his mother and father were rare. Tonight had all of them on edge.

The rustling of the sheet snapped everyone's attention back to the bed. The girl's unharmed arm moved slightly on the white linen, then her fingers gripped the fabric, balling it in her fist.

Roady stepped closer to the bed, reached up and brushed back a strand of ebony hair that had fallen across her face. He gently tucked it behind her ear.

That odd feeling, the one Luke had experienced the night Roady came to tell him about the lumpy jaw, gnawed at his gut. The image of the door's lock bar and what it represented to him—his mother's abduction and her inability to save herself—filtered through his mind.

He swallowed, unable to drag his gaze from the girl's flawless olive skin and the black lashes that fanned over her high-set cheeks. There was something about her that pulled him to her like a magnet. Was that happening with his mother too? Was she reliving her captivity in the Cheyenne village? Surely that was what Flood was doing.

"Look," Charity said, leaning forward. "I think she's waking up."

Perhaps this scrapper would prove the doctor wrong. Luke hoped she would.

"There," Faith said. "Her eyelids fluttered. She's waking up. I'm sure of it."

Roady went down on one knee next to the bed. "Wake up," he said softly. Luke wasn't the only one mesmerized. "Wake up. You're safe. No one'll hurt you."

Like the wings of a hummingbird, her eyelids fluttered again, this time for all to see. His mother moved to the side of the bed next to Roady. She reached out and gently ran a moist cloth over the girl's forehead, then smoothed down her hair.

"Wake up, Indian princess," his mother crooned, taking in every aspect of their visitor with a careful eye. "Wake up and tell us who you are. And why you're here."

When she opened her eyes, Luke couldn't look away. Her steady gaze—totally devoid of any fear—went around the faces until she came to his. She swallowed, blinked a few times, then, much to his surprise, the corner of her lips twitched, as if she were trying to smile.

Roady shifted, and she looked at him. "Hello," he said. She took him in, then turned back to Luke.

"Who are you?" his mother asked. Then she did the strangest thing, something she'd never done, ever, in his recollection. She spoke several Indian words. The girl turned her head, seeking the source of their origin.

Chapter Seventeen

Charity sucked in a breath when the peculiar words came from her mother's mouth. Of course the whole family knew the story of how her mother had been abducted as a young woman, barely over the age of nineteen. How she'd spent a year in a Cheyenne camp before Flood located her and bartered for her release. How she'd come home pregnant by her Indian husband, and several months later Luke was born.

To Charity's knowledge, her mother had never spoken about her captivity to anyone—surely the memories were just too painful. The topic was off-limits. Over the years, Charity had wondered all sorts of things but had never been brave enough to ask anyone, not even Luke. As time passed, she'd tucked her curiosity away, resigned that her mother had no intention of ever telling anyone.

Charity couldn't stop herself from glancing at her father's stricken face, and then at Luke's.

"Mother," Matt said in an abnormal, strangled voice, alarming Charity even more. What would this girl's sudden appearance do to her family? Seemed no one was immune to the pain etched on their parents' faces. "You're tired. Let Father take you home." He stepped forward and took her arm, but she gently pulled free.

"I'm fine, Matthew, and I'm staying. I don't need to be coddled, so please just stop."

The tension in the room made Charity want to disappear. Run out the door with Brandon and be alone with him in the moonlight. She'd never felt such division between everyone at the same time—all caused by three foreign words. Not even when Luke had pressed his difference into everyone's faces, day after day. Defiant. Belligerent. Begging anyone to bring up his half-breed heritage and give him a reason to fight. Sometimes he'd pushed so hard, his brothers would fight him until their pa broke things up, but they never did what he was after, which was to call him a half-breed.

Thank God Faith had come into his life. It seemed after he'd met her and they married, that whole part of his past was put to rest. He seemed so much happier, content.

Now, this Indian girl would dredge up all that unpleasantness.

And Flood. Charity didn't know how their father would handle the situation. Her heart broke for him the most.

In halting sounds, the girl uttered a few words. Claire leaned down and picked up her palm. With her eyes, she asked her to repeat what she'd just said.

"I believe her name is Fox something," Claire said matter-of-factly. "Fox Sitting, maybe Fox Moving. I'm not sure. It's been many years since I've heard the Cheyenne tongue. I do believe I got the first word correct, for I remember it distinctly because of a robe I made—" She closed her mouth quickly and kept her gaze on the hurt girl.

Her mother was so straightforward with all of this, her soft side all but gone. Charity inched closer to Brandon and he put his arm around her shoulder, bolstering her heart. In the other room, Holly started to cry and Faith immediately excused herself and left.

The girl tried again, this time more slowly. Then she said something else. Her mother shook her head, as if she didn't understand that either. With great effort, the girl took her hand from Claire's and made a sign.

Claire tipped her head.

The girl signed again, and this time pointed at Luke. Everyone in the room turned to look at him. Her brother's expression masked, but something in his eyes made her blanch.

A second ticked by and then Claire sucked in a deep breath. She covered her mouth with her hand, just staring at the wounded girl for several long moments before lifting her gaze to the others. "Brother," she finally said, and then sagged back into Matthew's strong embrace.

The girl nodded.

Flood, still halfway out the bedroom door, looked as if he couldn't decide if he was coming or going.

"Luke is her brother," Claire whispered.

Shocked, Charity searched Luke's face. He just stood there staring at the girl on the bed, who stared back at him. Now the resemblance jumped out like a slap in the face. Luke's dark hair wasn't quite as black as hers, but their olive-colored skin and gorgeous, mysterious eyes were a match if she'd ever seen one. *Luke resembles her more than he does me.* This Fox Something was as much his sister as she was. Charity and Luke shared a common mother, and this Indian girl and Luke shared a common father.

Pain sliced Charity's heart. All these years, she'd been Luke's prized little sister, as if she and Luke had an invisible bond between them that the rest of the family didn't share.

She the only sister, he the only half-breed. As horrible as that sounded, it was the truth. She'd reveled in that difference all these years. Now Luke had another sister. One who resembled him much more closely.

"B-broher." The girl's pronunciation was off, but there was no mistaking what she'd said. She looked around, unsure for the first time. Her lips wobbled.

"Luke?" Roady said, his brow questioning. "Aren't you going to say hello?"

Luke swallowed and stepped forward. He regarded his mother. She made a sign with her hand, and he slowly followed suit.

Instantly, the girl began signing back. She moved her hand slowly, then looked at Claire to see if she had caught her meaning.

"She says hello. Says it's medicine—good medicine," she corrected, "that the two of you are finally meeting. Says she's wanted to come see her great white brother for many seasons."

Flood turned and left the room.

The sound of him descending the staircase was like a death knell to Charity's heart.

"Are you all right, sweetheart?" Brandon whispered into her ear. "You're shaking like a leaf. You want me to take you home?"

Shaking like a leaf? An earthquake was mild compared to what twisted her gut. Her whole world had been snatched out from under her feet, tilted sideways, and then turned upside down. Her brother ripped away and her father's heart shattered.

Never before had she seen that look in her pa's eyes. He was a brave man, powerful and self-reliant. But this was one demon he couldn't fight, couldn't protect himself from the torment of knowing his wife had lived with another man for a whole year while her small sons back home cried for their mama. This girl must look a lot like her father, because she'd never seen that look in her mother's eyes either.

"No, not yet," Charity whispered back.

Brandon pulled her closer. "You just say the word."

"She's getting tired," Claire said. "We don't want to wear her out. She needs rest to recover more quickly."

As Claire turned, the girl reached out and grabbed her wrist. She made a few more signs.

Charity's mother shook her head and the girl tried again.

"Fox D...Danc-ing," the girl said.

Her mother smiled. "Her name is Fox Dancing." She signed back to the girl, who smiled and then closed her eyes.

Matt and Mark escorted their wives out of the room. Brandon stopped at the foot of the bed. Charity didn't want to leave Luke's side. Roady edged out of the room, his hat still in his hands. He stopped in the hall, looking back in.

Charity gave Luke's hand a tug. "What are you thinking?" she asked quietly when he looked down at her.

He rubbed a palm over his face and shrugged. "Life has just taken an interesting turn." His gaze cut to Brandon. "My brother-in-law-to-be is thinking Fox Dancing is the culprit who killed the calf in Pine Grove. And I'd have to agree with him. Her injured arm would explain the wobbly arrow wounds Sheriff Huxley observed. We'll pay restitution to the rancher involved and hope that satisfies him, but I don't think they're going to like that an Indian who is supposed to be on a reservation has turned up here. And is killing stock. It may stir up trouble."

That startled her. She'd forgotten about the trouble in Pine Grove.

"But what about you, Luke?" Charity asked. "How do you feel about all this?" He was her main concern. All the rest would work itself out the way it was supposed to. Luke had been hurt and angry for so long. She didn't want to see him slip back into his morose moods.

He gave her a tender smile. "Don't worry about me, Char. Ma and Flood are going to need us now more than ever."

She nodded. "Surely Pa will understand Mother hasn't made this happen. As hard as it's going to be on him, it will be more difficult for her, with the memories of her captivity for all those months."

"Just keep what I said in mind when you get back to the ranch. Be patient."

Charity snuck a glance at her mother, still gazing at Fox Dancing as if no one else were in the room. "I will."

Faith came back into the room and went to Luke's side. "Should I put the kettle on for tea?"

He shook his head. "I'm sure everyone would rather go home." He kissed her temple. "And I'm going to make sure my mother is one of them."

Chapter Eighteen

A huge buck moon lit the horse corrals and barn as Brandon led Charity through a copse of trees. They emerged into a meadow lush with thick Montana grass and flowers, in bloom all around. When they'd left Luke's house for the ranch, Flood had been waiting in moody silence in the wagon for Claire and Charity, having already taken the others home.

No one said a word as he helped them into the conveyance. Brandon mounted up and followed alongside, back to the main ranch house, feeling the edgy tension on his shoulders like a thick fog. When they arrived, Charity's parents had said their good-nights and disappeared inside to go to bed.

Brandon tugged on her hand and Charity turned into his waiting arms. The cool night air eased away his tense thoughts. They stood that way for a few minutes in silence, him just enjoying the feel of her finally in his embrace. He kissed her temple and ran his hands down her arms. Her stray hairs tickled his face. He'd never tire of the feel of her.

"What're you thinking, sweetheart? You have me worried."

With a sigh, she turned and rested her back against his chest to gaze up at the moon. He cocooned her in his warmth, trying to give her the support she needed. Time to gather her thoughts after the troubling evening. Everyone knew Mrs. McCutcheon's history—to a point. This couldn't be easy for any of them.

"I don't know what to think. I'm confused. And worried. My parents have never acted so peculiar. Pa's despondent, and Ma… I don't know what she is. Defiant? Driven? What?" With a sob, she turned back to face him, burying herself in his arms. Her clean lavender scent made him close his eyes. Another sob followed, then the wetness of her tears on his neck.

"Shh, honey. It's not all that bad. It's just different. Think of it as your family's growing. I'd love to discover family I didn't know I had."

He'd rarely seen Charity cry true tears in all the years he'd known her. He'd seen her fit to be tied. Embarrassed. And cry out of frustration when she couldn't have her way, but never tears of true sadness or uncertainty.

"I'm sure everyone will get over the shock by tomorrow and things will feel a whole lot better."

She shook her head. "I don't think so. Not for my pa. Fox Dancing is a constant reminder of what my mother underwent at the hands of that girl's father—*Luke's father*. I can't even imagine what he's feeling right now. This can only bode trouble. We all knew about my mother's suffering, but we never, ever talked about it. Now the whole thing is right in front of our faces."

Brandon took her hand and walked out farther into the field. He shrugged out of his light jacket and placed it on the ground. "Want to sit a while?"

He still needed to tell her about his plans. Kansas City was never far from his mind. How he'd do that, now that her emotions were so fragile, he hadn't a clue.

She seemed uncertain. "They might come looking for us."

He shook his head. "I don't think so. Not tonight."

In a swoosh of fabric, Charity sat, pulling her pretty green party dress to the side to make room for him. "You're right. What am I thinking? Me compromising myself out in the dark is the furthest thing from their minds now."

He lowered himself down beside her and drew her back into his arms. He couldn't stop a chuckle at her overdramatic simplification of the situation.

"Don't be silly. You're the first thing in their minds and hearts—now and always. Especially with the wedding less than a month away."

She made a sound of unbelief her throat, then she shrugged.

"That sounded pretty self-centered, and that wasn't my aim. I just want things to be good for my parents, and Luke too. *Do* you think that girl had anything to do with killing that calf in Pine Grove?"

"Probably everything to do with it. When I finally found some tracks, they led me here—to her."

"She'll get in trouble."

He nodded. "Luke's assumption that they'll just be able to make restitution may not be the case. But we'll have to wait and see. Just because she's Cheyenne and she was in the barn, doesn't make her guilty of that crime. Could be coincidence. There's too little evidence to say either way until she's better and we can talk to her."

"But if she did, what will happen to her?"

"You know the answer to that, Charity. She'll have a trial. But it's way too soon to be thinking about anything like that."

She jerked her gaze to his, and her hand found his forearm. "Being Indian, she may not get a fair trial."

He cupped her upturned face, the sight of her filling his soul. "I've learned years ago it doesn't help anything to jump to conclusions. We'll wait and keep an open mind until more is discovered. There could be several scenarios out there that have nothing to do with Fox Dancing."

He lowered his lips toward hers, wanting to chase the fear from her eyes. "Now I want a little time with my girl." Desire snaked through his veins at the warmth of her lips, so soft and innocent.

Charity McCutcheon could act as tough as she liked, but underneath her bravado, she was still a young girl. Sheltered by her family's love. The memory of the hayloft in Texas, where she'd shown him just how passionate a woman she was, fueled his blood.

Gently, he lowered her back into the fragrant grass, amid the lowing of cattle and the cry of a night bird. The moonlight washed over them like a wave, feeding his desire to touch her, hold her. With one hand, he traced the soft curve of her cheek, taking in her beauty, and then he kissed his way down her neck, marveling at its smoothness. His heart's tempo galloped off. They kissed until they were breathing hard and he knew he had to ease up.

"Brandon, I love you," she whispered as he drew away. "I wish we'd gotten married last week. Then we'd already be man and wife in all ways." She ran her hand down the front of his shirt, her fingers leaving a trail of fire through the fabric. "I need you so much tonight." Her teeth snagged her bottom lip for a moment, as if uncertain, then she said, "I'm willing."

Her face was only inches from his. If she was this beautiful after only a few kisses, he could only image her transformation after their first night together. As much as he wanted the same thing, he would not let their first time happen in a horse pasture. Or disrespect her parents' trust in him. But a voice in his head said that if they consummated their love right now, it would ensure she'd go anywhere with him. That she wouldn't call off the wedding once she knew his intentions.

He'd never loved her as much as he did in that moment. "Charity," he whispered. "Not yet, sweetheart. I want our first time to be in a big bed in some fancy hotel. I've already decided not to spend our first night at my house—as cozy as it is. We'll go somewhere else. Have a honeymoon."

Don't do it, Brandon, his conscience cautioned him. *I see where you're going, and it's not something you want to do. Don't mislead her even for a second.*

She went up on her elbow. "Have a honeymoon? Where would we go? Pine Grove? Or even Bozeman. We could ride over to Waterloo and go by train."

He pulled her back down and nuzzled her neck. "I was thinking somewhere even better."

"Where?" Her voice held a note of disbelief, excitement.

"How would you like to go to Kansas City?"

"Kansas City?"

The blood swooshed in Brandon's ears, as if he faced the gun barrel of a hardened outlaw. Tonight's conversation was indeed that grave.

"But we just got back from Texas," she said, placing small kisses around his lips. "What's this about, Brandon?"

Charity's fingers stilled, and she pulled them from Brandon's hair at the nape of his neck. A flutter deep in her belly made her long to pull him closer. She hated to change the subject from kissing, but Brandon's talk of a honeymoon far from home had come out of nowhere. A little confused, she said, "Why would you want to go to Kansas City?"

Instead of answering her question, he leaned forward and pressed his lips to her neck, making her shiver. He tried to gather her closer.

"Oh no, you don't, you sly dog." She laughed. "You're trying to distract me—which isn't hard to do. You can't make me forget my question. It can't be done."

She felt him shake his head. He sat up and brought her with him. "I guess you're right. Why Kansas City?" he repeated, as if she had indeed forgotten in the span of two seconds. "Just thought it might make you happy."

She knew Brandon better than that. The whole way home in the stage, he'd complained about the stuffy air, his clothes sticking to his warm skin, the bad food at the stage stops. He'd sworn that once he got back to Y Knot he wasn't going anywhere far for a good long time. That was only a few days ago. What had transpired to change all that?

One of the cowhands' laughter floated out over the field from the bunkhouse. The moon, still large and orangey pink, hung low over the far mountains; it was a sight to see. She'd remember this day for the rest of her life.

Brandon's face was solemn as he gazed at the moon.

"Brandon, you're scaring me."

He turned and smiled. "Nothin' to be frightened about. And nothin' we can't work through."

At his words, Charity stilled. This sounded serious. Not some silly whim. She didn't want more trouble on top of what had landed in their laps tonight. She wanted to know, and yet she didn't. With a gentle touch of her fingers and a leap of faith, she turned him to face her.

"Tell me," she whispered, feeling as if she'd just stepped backward off a high cliff.

He sighed. "The day we got home from Texas, I had a post waiting for me in the office. From a federal marshal in—"

"Kansas City," she finished.

He nodded. His thumb skimming across the top of her hand did little to calm her nerves. "Months ago, I learned this marshal would be hiring two new deputies. I've known Timberlake from when I was a kid, when I lost my parents. You and I were arguing, and you'd sworn you didn't want to see my face ever again. It seemed like things between us were never going to go anywhere, no matter how much I hoped."

She pulled away and looked at him. He'd told her he had no recollection of his past. That he'd been so young when he lost his parents, but maybe that wasn't the case at all. That had always felt a little peculiar to her, but she'd not questioned him—didn't want to cause more pain where she could already see it lingering in his eyes.

"Charity?"

She tried to push away her hurt that he'd used their on-again, off-again relationship as an excuse to do something so important. Besides, they always argued. It made the making up so sweet. She'd never had doubts about them. Their affection for each other had always been true. At least, that was what she'd believed.

"I was just angry enough at the time to think I didn't have a snowflake's chance in July to marry you. But then you ran off to Denver and Texas, and I went after you. Time passed, and I forgot all about it until the day we arrived back into Y Knot."

It took a moment for his comment to register. She'd been expecting some silly answer that would make her laugh, like *I knew you've been dreaming of time away*. Or *I have tickets to the Kansas City Opera six nights in a row*—something, anything, other than the truth. She swallowed down the fear clogging her throat.

She'd been right and her mother had been wrong! Brandon *had* been acting abnormal. He'd been torn over their engagement and had other things on his mind. She hadn't imagined it at all. She knew him better than anybody. She'd never second-guess her intuition about him again.

"Charity, say something."

"I don't know what to say. You made a major, life-changing decision without even considering what it would do to us? Without talking to me? I'm astounded, but I'm also heartbroken. Do you even still want to get married?"

"Charity." He pulled her to him, but she pushed against his chest. "You know I do. You know it!"

"I don't know anything anymore. I don't understand about this lawman, Brandon. You've never said anything about him before, or wanting to be a marshal." It was more than hurt, it was shock—and a good dose of anger. All these years, they'd never discussed marriage, but she'd been firmly committed to Brandon in her mind. All her brothers had known how she felt. She thought Brandon understood how serious she was about him. Maybe she'd been wrong.

"I've never told you this before, but when I was just a boy—"

"Charity!" It was her pa's voice, and he sounded mad. "Charity, where are you?"

She rushed to stand, but Brandon grasped her arm. "Wait, let me finish. I have to explain why it means so much to me. When I was—"

"Brandon?" Claire McCutcheon called. "You bring Charity in this instant. You're not married yet!"

Her mother's normally pleasant voice sounded strained and harsh.

"I've got to get back before the whole bunkhouse gets sent out on a search party."

In reality, she couldn't bear to hear what Brandon was about to say. Here they were again. Another reason to wait— argue, have hurt feelings. Another round of arguments, making up, only to start all over again. Perhaps their future wasn't written in the stars, like she'd believed her whole life. Maybe it was time to let Brandon go.

Chapter Nineteen

Morning came early. Luke climbed out of the warm bed in the dark and pulled the blanket up around Faith's shoulder before slipping into his pants and a shirt. He couldn't lie in bed one minute longer. Too many thoughts were rolling around in his head like prickly pears in a barrel. He'd been awake for hours, since before Holly's two o'clock feeding. When his daughter's small cries began, it wasn't but a moment before Faith crept quietly out of bed and pulled on her wrapper. This was her favorite feeding, she'd told him more than once. The house was dark and quiet and she had Holly all to herself.

He'd listened as she cooed to the babe, picked her up, then crossed the floor to the dresser to change her soggy drawers. Then they sat in the rocker for a good forty-five minutes. When Holly was finished, they'd played for a while, with Faith's whispers and Holly's gurgles making a happy sound in the dark. Every once in a while, he'd hear Faith laugh softly, then speak in that way only a mother could do to a babe in the wee hours of the night.

He'd learned a lot of things since becoming a father.

As he'd listened, he'd been thinking about Fox Dancing. The sight of the Cheyenne sister he hadn't known he'd had, lying in that bed, so close to death, had rocked him. He guessed most of the family in the room had probably thought he was upset with her arrival at his ranch. It wasn't that at all, although he did worry about how his pa and mother would handle the situation, how they would navigate through this sudden disruption in their marriage. It wouldn't be easy. Especially after his mother had confided in him last year that her life with his real father hadn't been horrible, and that her feelings for him had grown during their time together. At first, he'd been mystified at Fox Dancing's appearance, then filled with wonder. Here was his chance to learn more about his father. Here was the gift of another sister.

Luke carefully closed the bedroom door. He briefly looked in on Dawn as he made his way down the hall toward the stairs. She slept soundly, worn out from the shindig yesterday. In the upper hallway, he opened the last door to confirm Colton was indeed fine. Across the hall from his son's room was where Fox Dancing slept. He wondered if she was awake.

He'd sat by her side most of the night, then around one had been relieved by Roady. Tired, he'd trudged off to bed. Faith had offered to take a shift, but with Holly and Dawn to attend to, Luke insisted she get her sleep.

Taking the knob in his hand, he carefully opened the door. The room was quiet. Roady's legs stretched out in front of the chair, crossed at the ankles. Limp arms rested on his stomach, and his chest made a pillow for his chin. He took a deep breath that wasn't quite a snore.

When Luke's gaze moved to his sister, he was surprised to see her eyes open and watching him. He nodded and smiled. Three steps brought him to Roady's side. He nudged his shoulder and Roady opened his eyes.

"Morning," Luke said low.

"Is it?" Roady replied. "I just now fell asleep."

Luke nodded. "Indeed. Fox Dancing is awake. I guess she's stronger than the doctor thought." He sent a reassuring look to Fox Dancing, who regarded him with curious eyes.

Roady sat up straight and ran his hand through his rumpled hair.

"How is she?"

Roady shrugged. "She still doesn't trust me. After you left last night, we pretty much had a staring contest. She was tired, but she didn't dare close her eyes until I did. When I finally caught on, I closed my eyes and pretended I was asleep. It wasn't but two shakes of a lamb's tail before she was out like a lamp."

"I appreciate you staying."

His longtime friend grunted, then his signature grin split his face. "What's for breakfast? I feel like my gut's been empty for a week. I think I was dreaming of a platter of steak and eggs with a side of potatoes, and a waffle."

"A platter, huh? That's good, because that's partly what you'll be getting from the leftovers from the barn dance last night. I'm on my way to the kitchen now to put the coffee on." He went to the opposite side of the bed and placed a palm on Fox Dancing's head. She closed her eyes at the contact. She was still running hot. As much as he wanted to feel some relief, it was too soon to think his little sister was out of the woods just yet.

Roady stood and stretched. A pained expression crossed his face when he twisted his back one way and then the other. "What time is it anyway?"

"Almost five thirty. Faith would've been up by now, but she just got back into bed an hour ago. I want to have the house warm before she does make it down." He chuckled and shook his head. "Seems Holly thought it was her time to play after her parents and all the neighbors had their fun last night. That little sprite knows how to charm the socks off a horse."

"Fine. I'm coming with you." Roady preceded him to the door.

It took a few minutes to get a fire going in the kitchen stove, and a handful more to perk the coffee. Soon, the brew's savory aroma filled the room.

"What do you make of her, Luke?" Roady asked, taking the mug of coffee he offered.

"It's a shock, all right, but not to me. Ever since hearing the truth about my heritage, I've wondered if I had brothers and sisters out there somewhere. Now I know."

Roady regarded him with his stoic gaze. "Seems your pa's taking it pretty hard. It was mighty uncomfortable last night when your ma surprised us talking Cheyenne. I'll tell you, my jaw almost hit the floor when the first word popped out." He shook his rumpled head. "Stands to reason, though, that she'd know the language. She was there for about a year."

Luke tossed him an aggravated look as he sliced a roast, laying strips of beef in the hot skillet. "You sure seem to know a lot about it."

Their ranch foreman shrugged. "That's not my fault. Every time a new man is hired on, the talk goes around the bunkhouse. It's natural, Luke. The men don't mean any disrespect to your mother. Why, every single one would risk death to keep her safe."

The butter in the hot skillet turned brown as the meat fried. Luke pushed it around with a fork, understanding what Roady said was the truth. "I know—"

He glanced over when Colton walked into the room. He nodded at the boy before replying low so Colton couldn't hear as he took a crock of milk from the icebox. "Still don't make it any easier to think your mother is the topic of bunkhouse talk."

Fox Dancing lay in the softness of the snowy cloths of the bed as she watched the men leave the room. She marveled over the feel of the fabric. Normally, she'd wake to the prickly softness of animal skin next to her nakedness. This material was smooth and cool, almost wet feeling. At the thought, she glanced down in alarm, checking to see if they'd stripped her in her weakness and taken away her buckskins. Relief washed through her when she saw she was still dressed in her breeches, but her shirt had been changed for one of soft cotton.

Brother sun sent beams of yellow light streaming through the sparkling glass window; they landed on the covering of her bed. The window at the Indian agency was so gummy with smudges, she'd hardly understood they were for peering through. This was beautiful. She slowly reached out and touched the shimmery glow of warmth.

Thinking of her brother, satisfaction slid through her veins like baby fish in the streams. She'd accomplished her quest. Met him in the flesh. Her father and grandfather would be proud of her. Making the trip alone had been a great accomplishment. She'd proven herself worthy.

She wondered what Painted Bear Stone would think when he knew what she'd done. She pictured his laughing face—and then him scowling, trying unsuccessfully to frighten her. Her heart warmed a little, recalling all the times he'd been only one step behind, thinking himself her protector and guardian. *Does he wonder where I am? What I'm doing? If I've gone to the great hunting ground in the sky? Does he—*

She slammed her eyes shut, appalled with the course her thoughts had taken. She didn't care what that proud, strutting brave thought. Once he'd asked her father to marry her, everything had changed. She'd never marry any man! Especially not Painted Bear Stone.

She turned her mind to Luk and how tall he was, and the acceptance she'd seen in his eyes. There had been something else there too.

Trying to distract herself from her musings, she gazed around the room. A lantern burned on a wooden cabinet against the wall. She'd never been inside a white man's home. Just the shanty they called the Indian Officer's Trading Post, when she snuck onto the reservation. That was where she heard more of the white tongue and became familiar with some of the things they kept in their dwellings.

The darkness of that malevolent place always brought an edginess to her heart. Doom saturated everything inside— permeated her brothers and sisters who waited for their week's allotment of old, decaying food. Their spirits had been sucked from their bodies after they'd given in and moved to the pitiful piece of land the whites had so generously given them.

Her father's village was one of the last to refuse to be moved. Because of it, the angry white dogs were always hunting them. Stealing her people away one by one, to lock them away on the reservations, where the dry, crippled land was devoid of any game and her people had to live on handouts.

Hunger and death were synonymous with a broken heart.

Fox Dancing's stomach let out a loud protest when a warm, enticing smell floated underneath her door. She closed her eyes and took it in, her mouth welling up with saliva. If she had the strength, she'd climb from this bed and search out the source. It had been days since she'd had more than a bite of jerky. And where was her horse? She couldn't remember where she'd left her. Or her bow and quiver.

There was no question as to who the woman was last night, the one who had known the Cheyenne words. Luk's mother, and still beautiful. Her father had told her that Luk's mother was the strongest woman he'd ever known. She'd taken the gauntlet with the courage of a bear. She'd not been cowed when the others pulled her hair and slapped her face.

Her mistreatment stopped when she was given to Fox Dancing's father, Netchiwaan, an important warrior of the village, with two wives already and a handful of children. Her father used to smile fondly when he'd shared those stories, and Fox Dancing got the impression she was the wife of his heart.

Others told her how her father had grieved after Luk's mother had gone away. He left the village for almost a full year. When he came back, others said that he'd changed.

A squeal of laughter made Fox Dancing open her eyes. The sound was followed by the calm, soothing voice of the child's mother, quieting her. Footsteps, and then a tiny scratching, alerted Fox Dancing to someone outside her door. The round doorknob turned and the door came open a small way.

Squinting, she didn't see anything at first. Not until she lowered her gaze to below the level of the bed. An eye peered through the crack. The eye blinked.

A child. Happiness lifted her soul as if it had wings. The eye widened when the child noticed he or she had been spotted. Fox Dancing willed her mouth into a smile.

"Come in," she said softly in her Indian tongue. "Come keep me company."

The eye blinked several times more before the door opened a little farther. As she had suspected, it was the little girl she'd caught a glimpse of last night. She was holding some sort of toy, she presumed, for it resembled the dolls her people made by sewing together scraps of deerskin and stuffing them with grass.

The child looked to be about three or four years old. This must be her brother's daughter, the one her father had seen on his last trip, when she was just a baby. Her hair sparkled like the morning sun, and her rosy cheeks and bright blue eyes said she was robust with good health.

The girl came forward. She stopped several arm's lengths away from the bed, so Fox Dancing couldn't get hold if she so wanted. Smart. She'd not be caught unawares.

Fox Dancing smiled and wiggled the fingers of her good arm. That drew a small smile from her. She looked at the ceiling and then wiggled her nose. That won a soft giggle. A moment later, Luk came through the door with a tray in his hands.

Luk drew up short when he spotted her. His smile ebbed away. "What are you doing in here, darlin'?"

The child pointed to Fox Dancing lying in the bed. "I wanna see the Indian princess." Her head tipped to the side. "Where's her crown wiff jewels?"

Amusement, not anger, flashed across her brother's eyes. He was patient. Kind with his offspring. He set the tray on the dresser and scooped his daughter into his arms, giving her a kiss on her cheek. A moment later he set her back on the floor. "Run along to the kitchen." The girl scampered out the door.

Luk retrieved the tray and set it on Fox Dancing's lap, gesturing to the food. "Can you eat on your own?" He made some gestures of bringing the food to his mouth.

She nodded.

The food on the tray looked strange but smelled wonderful. She was doing all she could to be polite and not grasp a handful and stuff it into her mouth. Life here was different, and she hadn't been farther than this room. What would it be like when she could get up to explore? What stories would she have to take back—stories that, had she married Painted Bear Stone, she would never have known?

Chapter Twenty

Tuesday morning was Brandon's first opportunity to ride out to the Heart of the Mountains. He was anxious to straighten things out with Charity. He needed a chance to explain his reasons for wanting to go to Kansas City. Since their ill-fated walk in the moonlight, he'd not been able to think of anything except the hurt in her eyes and the anger in her voice that she'd been unable to disguise. For all he knew, she was fed up with their unpredictable relationship. If she were, he could hardly blame her.

At the ranch, he dismounted and tied his horse at the hitching rail in front of the bunkhouse. He strode to the front door of the main house and knocked, more nervous than he'd ever been in his life. Had she said anything to anyone else?

It wasn't but a moment before Esperanza came to the door and greeted him. The housekeeper wore her usual smile and happy glint in her expressive dark eyes.

"I will let Miss Charity know you are here."

It was early for a visit, only six o'clock, but he hadn't wanted to miss her going out to the cattle. This had to be dealt with today. It was already two days overdue.

The maid hurried up the stairs.

Claire emerged from the kitchen and pulled up short. "Brandon. Good morning. What a nice surprise." It wasn't her usual over-the-top warm welcome. Of course Charity would have shared the information with her mother. Then again, maybe it was still Luke's new sister that affected her so. He remembered Flood's reaction.

He turned his hat in his hands. An abnormal drop of sweat trickled down his temple. "Good morning, Mrs. McCutcheon."

"Have you eaten?" Claire asked.

"Actually, no." He glanced up at the staircase, where Esperanza descended. "I wanted to be sure to catch Charity before she went to work. I hope my barging in unannounced isn't a problem."

Claire tipped her head. "A problem? That's an odd thing to say. You've been eating breakfast with us for years. Why would it be barging in now, especially since you and Charity are engaged?"

He shrugged, wishing he felt more relieved that Charity hadn't told her. She smiled and patted his back, then hurried away. "I'll get another setting," she called as she disappeared into the kitchen.

Brandon paced to the big window, wishing Charity would hurry up. He didn't want to get caught with the whole family before they spoke in private. He glanced up the stairs again. A few loud voices from outside made his decision for him. Taking the stairs two at a time, he reached the second floor and disappeared around the wall just as the front door opened. He approached Charity's door and knocked.

"I'll be right there, Esperanza."

The sound of her voice was a balm to his hurting soul. He would have come sooner, but the poker tournament at the saloon had turned into a brawl and he had two fellas locked up.

"It's me, Charity. Open up."

The door opened instantly. "Brandon?"

She was dressed in her riding clothes. The ponytail hanging down her back reminded him of their time in Texas. He wished they could turn back the hands of time.

Clearly, she hadn't expected his arrival. Her puffy red eyes contradicted the straight, stubborn line to her lips.

"What are you doing up here? I was just on my way down."

"I wanted to talk to you in private. Downstairs is ready to explode with people coming inside to eat. We need to work this out before another day passes. I don't want to sit and make small talk with your parents and brothers when the whole time all I want is to kiss you." He leaned in to kiss her lips, but she pulled back just far enough that all he got was air. Embarrassed, he straightened. "Charity?"

"What do you expect of me, Brandon? Tell me, because I don't know. One moment, you ask me to marry you, and the next, you tell me you're moving to Missouri."

"I didn't say I was moving to Missouri."

When he tried to enter the room, she held him off with her hand to his shoulder. "Father will be angry if he finds you in my room. I don't want to add to his problems."

A bit irked, Brandon took her wrist. The least she could do was let him explain. "Fine. Then come over to Mark's old room. You can sit in the chair and I'll stand. That's innocent enough."

He didn't wait for her response, but pulled her like a cranky colt across the hall. He left the door ajar, just enough to keep her parents happy in case they were to venture up.

She sat in the big leather chair by the window and looked at him, waiting for him to speak his mind. "With everyone downstairs, don't you think this could wait?"

"Maybe, but I feel the ticking clock."

She lifted her chin and shifted in her seat. He was in for a battle.

"Fine, then. Go on and say what you have on your mind. I won't stop you."

He'd rehearsed the lines on the ride over here this morning, but faced with her clear blue eyes that had always held so much love for him—and still did even in her anger—the words evaporated right out of his head. This was Charity he stood to lose. He better get his act together, and get it together quick.

"I don't know why I didn't mention the job before now. Maybe it was because I believed I didn't stand a chance of getting it. Or maybe I was afraid this would happen."

"You still intend to go?"

That shocked him. He'd never suggested he'd given up on his chance at deputy marshal. "That's why I'm here. I have to leave tomorrow to make it on time. It's just an interview, but I want you to go with me, Charity. We can ride into town and get married by—" He stopped. Reverend Crittlestick had left town yesterday and wouldn't be back until next week. That only left Jack Jones. "Jack."

She shook her head, every hurt she'd ever felt wafting across her face. He didn't want to add another to the list. "You never answered my question from the other night. How could you apply for such a job if you thought we had any future together at all? As hard as I try, I don't understand that one bit."

"Be reasonable, Charity. Just say yes and marry me today so we can get on with our lives. We'll have a nice time." He held out his hand in supplication. He was still dying for a kiss, but didn't want to go there until he felt her soften.

"Reasonable? Like you were, Brandon?" Her voice took on a hard clip. "You made a life-changing decision without a by-your-leave to me? To the woman you claim you love? The job certainly means more to you than I do. And if not that, the moment you received that letter, you should have told me. I'd been dancing around for days, as if on air, dreaming about my Prince Charming and the upcoming wedding."

Brandon strode to the window and looked out, wrangling with his anger. Yes, she was right. He should have mentioned it. Talked about it. But he hadn't. How many times over the years had she played tricks on him or told half truths? He'd been pretty darn patient, come to think of it.

"You don't want to go there, Charity. You were the one who ran off to Texas without telling a soul. That was unforgivable. I wasn't the only one scared to death for your safety, but your whole family. You could have been killed several times, or been forced to live a life you'd hate. Isn't the pot calling the kettle black?"

She bolted to her feet. "Is this how you win a conversation? By attacking me and bringing up past incidents that you said you had forgiven? You're just trying to draw the attention from what you've done and pin the guilt on me. Well, I'm not having it, Brandon. You can just go to Missouri, for all I care. Actually, I'm glad this whole chapter of my mixed-up life is over!"

Before he could catch her, she flew out of the room and he heard her footsteps descending the stairs.

The chatter downstairs stopped. He left the bedroom and pulled the door closed. He stopped in the hall, where he couldn't yet be seen. If there were any other way out of the house, he'd take it. He didn't care if it was cowardly.

Chapter Twenty-One

Charity rushed into the middle of family—her mother, Matthew, and Luke, and Roady was there too. Six place settings adorned the table. Again, no Pa. For the past two days he'd taken his breakfast and gone out riding before anyone else was up. And her mother, she could act all she wanted, but Charity could see her emotions simmering on her face every time her father walked into or out of the room. It hurt seeing the strain between them.

"No, thanks," Luke was saying to their mother. His brows arched when he caught sight of her. "Roady and I ate over at my place. We'll have coffee, though, before we start treating the cattle…"

He caught her by the shoulder when she tried to scoot by. "Char, is everything all right?"

Charity silenced the clamor in her mind by chomping down on the inside of her cheek. A tinny taste touched her tongue. "Fine, Luke."

All eyes shifted from her to the staircase, and tension filled the room. Brandon was on his way down.

"What's going on?" her mother asked. Her concerned gaze made Charity's insides freeze up.

So much for her acting abilities. When she was little, she'd have been able to pull this off with ease. But not now. Not with her entire life crashing down around her shoulders. Not with the three-foot knife that was slicing away at her heart. And especially not with Brandon in the same room.

She heard his footsteps, felt his presence behind her. If she could only turn back the hands of time, back to Texas when they were happy—without all these problems. Oh, why hadn't she married him then? Glancing into the kitchen, she longed to disappear out the back door.

"Morning, Brandon," Roady said. He looked around at everyone, a confused expression pinching his face. "You're out early."

"Had things to discuss with Charity." The hard edge of anger in his voice was new.

Her mother wrapped her arm around Charity's shoulder. "I wondered where you'd gone off to, Brandon. You two aren't…"

Unable to hold in her feelings any longer, Charity burst into tears. She pulled out from her mother's arm and raced back up the stairs. It didn't take but a second for Claire to follow behind.

Luke watched until Charity disappeared into the upper hall. Was this a case of jittery nerves caused by the upcoming wedding? It was possible, but by the look on Brandon's face, he'd bet it was a lot more than that.

With Charity and his mother gone, and him and Roady already having eaten, Matt was the only one to take a seat at the table. "I'll be with you men as soon as I wolf this down."

Esperanza's expression said she was not pleased with everyone deserting the meal.

Luke headed to the door, and Brandon and Roady followed him outside. Roady beat a fast retreat to the bunkhouse. "Let me know when you're ready to get started," he called to Luke.

Luke waited until Roady was well out of earshot. "What's going on *now*?"

Brandon looked away for several seconds. When he turned back, his gaze was flinty hard. "You just had to toss that in, didn't you?"

"Toss what in?"

"The 'now.' You and everyone else just love to throw that in our faces every chance you get. The fact that we seem to argue a lot."

Luke took a step back. "Hold on. I didn't mean anything by what I said. You're stewing for a fight, Brandon, but you won't get it from me."

Brandon didn't answer. He just looked off into the pasture as if he were contemplating some big issue. Surely Charity was being overly sensitive, the way women could be sometimes—a lot of the time, he corrected. Men just had to be on the lookout and know when to cut their losses. Pick their battles. Brandon had a lot to learn about the fairer sex.

"What's the problem? Is she insisting you wear some flowers in your hair at the wedding, or something similar? Talk to me. Maybe I can help."

When Brandon turned, the anger in his eyes startled Luke. "What?"

"It's nothing like that. Actually, I thought Charity might have already told you, but I can see now that I was wrong. She usually comes running to you for everything."

That comment went right up Luke's back. Why wouldn't she? She was his sister. He looked out for her. Then, now—and would continue to do so in the future. Nothing would change that, not even her getting married.

"I'm going to ignore you just said that, because I can see that you're fuming mad and upset. But you had no call. I hope Charity never stops coming to me for advice. Now, are you going to spit out what has you riled, or am I going to have to beat it out of you?" he said half-jokingly.

Brandon scoffed.

"Well? You being so close-mouthed leads me to the conclusion that Charity may be in the right and you in the wrong. Am I getting warm?"

"It's not like that. Neither is right or wrong. Just that I have a chance to be a federal deputy marshal, albeit a small chance, but I need to go to Kansas City. I want Charity to marry me and come along. Make a real honeymoon out of it."

Luke had to clench his jaw to keep it from falling open. Federal deputy marshal? Where had that idea come from? He'd never heard Brandon speak about leaving Y Knot. No wonder his sister was in a world of hurt.

"I can't believe what I'm hearing. This feels totally out of the blue."

"Maybe to you, but not to me. I've always had the desire."

"You just never mentioned it to anyone, least of all Charity?"

Brandon pointed a finger at Luke. "Does my job change her feelings for me? I thought it was me she was supposed to love, not where we lived or what I did to make a living."

"You're not being fair," Luke shot back.

Luke needed to remember his friend was hurting, but damn, this made him angry. He could see why it would throw

Charity into a panic. He believed she loved Brandon with her whole heart, but she also loved her family, and the ranch. Never in a million years had she expected that marrying Brandon would mean moving away.

"You're the first to know what this ranch and the family mean to her. When did you drop this on her? Today?"

They stood angry face to angry face. He couldn't push Brandon much more or they would end up in a fistfight. "Well? When did you tell her, Brandon? I can guarantee it wasn't at Cattlemen's. I would have been able to tell if she were struggling with something. She was happier that night than I've ever seen her."

"Saturday night after the party."

Luke shook his head. This was big. He didn't know how the two would work their way out of this one.

"I didn't know until the day we returned to Y Knot," Brandon said a little more calmly. "When I went to the office, Jack gave me the letter. Just because I have an interview, doesn't mean I'll get the job."

Luke gripped the back of his neck, working his tight muscles. Brandon just stood there watching him, and he didn't know how to respond. When a few seconds passed, Brandon started for his horse. "I need to get back to Y Knot. I have some prisoners that need tending."

"When are you leaving for Kansas City?" Luke asked, watching him retreat.

"Tomorrow morning."

"How long will you be gone?"

Brandon unwrapped his reins and turned his horse around to face him. "I don't know."

Chapter Twenty-Two

Twenty-four hours later, Charity, mounted on her palomino, trotted down Main Street with Luke riding by her side. Few people were out at the early hour. The clapboard buildings running down both sides of the street appeared shabbier since her return from Texas. She didn't like to think it.

When they passed the saloon, an upstairs window opened and Fancy Aubrey leaned out. "Morning, Luke." She smiled and waved, unmindful that she was only in her dressing gown and was putting on a show for the whole world to see. "Charity."

Luke waved back, and Charity nodded.

"That Fancy sure seems to get around," she couldn't stop herself from saying. The image Francis had planted in her mind of her and Brandon in close conversation now troubled her all the more.

"You sure you're up to this?" Luke asked. "He may already be gone. He didn't give me a time when he was pulling out."

"I'm sure. I won't be able to do a thing if Brandon and I don't finish what we started yesterday."

And it was true. She'd done a lot of soul searching last night. As much as it hurt, she only wanted what was best for Brandon. Her desire was for him to be happy. If Kansas City would do that, then so be it. They reined up in front of the sheriff's office.

Jack Jones walked out to greet them. "Morning, you two. You looking for Brandon?"

She nodded.

"If you hurry, you might still catch him. He left for his house just a few minutes ago and plans to leave straight from there. He's riding to Waterloo, where he'll catch the train."

"Thanks, Jack," Luke said.

Jack turned and went back inside.

Luke reached out before she turned her horse. He laid his hand on her forearm. "Stay calm. Don't let your temper get the best of you. I'll be waiting at the saloon and will go over to Lichtenstein's when the place opens up. Take as long as you need."

She nodded. Gathering her courage, she rode down the alley between the sheriff's office and Cattlemen's Hotel, frightened she hadn't made it in time. What if he'd already gone? Hadn't she learned anything in that death cell with the rattlesnake? Didn't she love Brandon above everything else?

"Charity!" Brandon said, surprised. His face lit with pleasure. She'd caught him just stepping through his front door, bulging saddlebags in his hands.

The happiness on his face brought a new burst of butterflies in her stomach. Maybe he hurt inside as much as she did. He rushed over and helped her dismount. When his hand grasped her arm, a flurry of tingles ignited in her belly. For a moment, they stood in silence, looking into each other's eyes.

"I wanted to see you before you left." That was all she could think of. *Really, I want to kiss you and feel your lips on mine.*

"I'm glad you came. I wanted to come back out to the ranch, but the men we had locked up were a handful. I couldn't leave Jack alone. They've all sobered up and have been released." His eyes dropped to her lips, but quickly returned to her eyes. Shame for pulling away from his kiss yesterday filled her. The memory had kept her awake long into the early morning. What she wouldn't give for that kiss right now.

She glanced over her shoulder. "Is there somewhere we can talk? I feel conspicuous standing out here."

"Sure, sure. Just let me get rid of this." He went to his horse and hefted the saddlebags over the back of the saddle and buckled them on.

He disappeared inside, then brought out two chairs and set them on the porch. They'd be out of view if someone looked down the alley from Main Street.

"Come sit down." He gestured with his hand.

For one instant, she let her thoughts run wild. He was so earnest. His strong, handsome profile did silly things to her heart. His hatless hair glistened in the sun. But it was his eyes that made her insides feel like melted butter. Here they were again, tiptoeing around each other. She wanted the intimacy back. The easiness, when she knew where she stood and so did he.

He smiled when she lowered herself into the plain, straight-back chair. "There. You good? Is that comfortable?"

He's trying so hard. When she nodded, he sat opposite her and waited for her to say something.

"I'm sorry about yesterday, Brandon." She didn't need a script. She'd say whatever came out of her heart. "The argument, not kissing you—and for running up to my room when I should have stayed and heard you out. You came all the way to the ranch. That was the least I could have done. Please forgive me."

He nodded as she spoke, as if he felt the same. "I'm sorry too, Charity. Yesterday didn't go at all like I planned. Not even close."

They stared at each other. Her mouth went dry. The depth of his sorrow was easy to see. "I don't really know what else to say, Brandon, except that I love you." *And want you to be happy.* "No matter what, that will always be true."

She dropped her gaze for a moment. Maybe he wasn't planning on coming back if he got the job, just staying on there and starting up. He probably didn't know what the marshal would want from him.

He leaned forward and tentatively took both her hands. His callused palms had never felt so good. His thumbs rubbed back and forth across her skin, and she had to swallow back her grief. "I know," he replied. "And I love you. I've been doing some hard thinking about what Luke had to say. How I wasn't being fair to you by dropping this in your lap after you had said yes to becoming my wife. I didn't want to believe it then because I was mad, but he was right. I don't know what I expected. I still don't."

Unable to stop herself, Charity slipped onto his lap. His arms immediately closed around her and he held her tight to his chest. She burrowed in closer, her face against his good-smelling, warm neck, and all their problems faded to the back of her mind. This was Brandon. Her protector. It was so good, so uplifting to be here in his arms, somewhere she thought she'd never be again. He was everything in the world to her.

"I'm sorry I hurt you, Charity," he said, running his hand down the back of her hair. "You deserve more than that. You deserve more than I can ever dream of giving you. Maybe this is for the best. Maybe—"

She pulled back to look into his face. "Don't you dare say another word. Have I ever said I want more than you can give me? No. Never. So don't say that now. That has nothing to do with where we are today."

"You're right, sweetheart," he replied. He gently took her chin and found her mouth with his own. The kiss was sweet, and apologetic. He cupped her face between his hands, taking his time moving his lips over hers, and she thought she'd die from the goodness of it.

"Do you want me to stay, Charity? I will if you say so."

She shook her head. This would be the hardest thing she'd ever done, but he had to be able to follow his dreams.

"No, if being a deputy marshal means that much to you, I'd never want to hold you back from your dreams. Later, you'd resent me for it and always wonder what would have happened if you'd tried. I insist that you go. I won't have it any other way."

"What about the wedding? Are you saying you'll wait?"

She shrugged. "We'll cross that bridge when you return." *If you return.*

Setting him free was like a broken bottle raking over her heart, but she had to do it. He'd not go if he thought she was going to be pining over his every move. "I think it's best if we don't upset everyone now. We'll tell them the wedding is still on for when you come home. That way, if it happens, no one will have worried unduly, and if it doesn't, at least their vexation will have been for a shorter amount of time."

"I never told you why this means so much to me, but I want to now, before I leave, so you can understand." He looked away, gathering his thoughts. "I'm sorry about not being truthful with you about my parents. I just couldn't tell anyone because of the guilt I felt—still do—about how they were killed. I was only a kid, but somehow I thought I should have been able to protect them from the outlaw who robbed and then killed them."

Unable to stop her reaction, she gasped. What a burden he'd held to himself. Charity could understand why, now that she knew. "Brandon, I'm not mad, just sorry for you. What you went through."

He nodded. A shadow in his eyes, one she'd never before seen, twisted her insides.

"My pa tossed me out of the moving wagon and into some bushes when he feared the worst was about to happen. But I was still close enough to see. After my mother gave the robber the little money they had, he shot them both. A moment later, a lawman came down the road. He quickly assessed the situation and took the outlaw down. His name was Timberlake. I never forgot the name. The memory and emotions, even the guilt, have bound me to him over the years. Now there may be a chance I could actually work with him and—"

She put her finger on his lips. "You don't have to say another thing. I totally understand why you'd be drawn there—and to the marshal. I do. And I wouldn't want anything else for you. You have to go and see how it feels." She meant every word, even if they were breaking her heart.

He kissed her again, and she could tell he was relieved. It wasn't the sad good-bye it had been before, but filled with a hope that he could sway her to move away with him when he took the marshal's job. Her heart thumped painfully in her breast. What would become of them? He wanted that job, there was no denying it.

Brandon ran his hand down the side of her face. "Thank you for coming, Charity. You'll never know what it means to me that we had a chance to talk this out. I feel a lot better."

"I think I do, Brandon," she said against his lips, one last time.

"I need to go, sweetheart, or I'll miss the train in Waterloo. As it is, I don't know if I'll make it."

Fear skittered around inside, threatening to bring tears to her eyes. She willed them away. She stood and pulled him to his feet. "You get going, then," she said, swallowing down a lump of sadness. "Don't worry about anything here. I'll make sure Jack Jones is doing his job."

"You just stay out at the ranch, so I won't worry over you. Hayden will be sure Jack toes the line until I get back."

If you get back.

He went over and retrieved Charity's horse and slung the reins over its neck. He helped her mount. "Is Luke in town with you?"

She nodded, almost too overcome with regret to pull this off. Somewhere she found the fortitude to say, "Yes. I'm meeting him over at Lichtenstein's."

"Good." He gazed up at her with so much love, she thought she might faint. "You give everyone out at the ranch my regards." He had his hand on her knee and she had the urge to pick it up and kiss it, but she knew he'd think she'd lost the last of her sanity.

He disappeared into his house and reappeared wearing his black Stetson. Locking the door, he strode over to his horse and mounted, spinning him around. He trotted back to Charity to kiss her again. "I just needed one more to get me through."

Choked up, she forced a little smile. "Get going. They won't hold that train for you forever, you know."

He laughed, then shook his head. She was sure he thought everything had worked out just fine.

"All right, I'm going, I'm going. You take good care of yourself. I'll miss you more than you'll ever know. Still wish you were coming along."

"I'll see ya when I see ya, Sheriff." Her throat burned so tight, she could hardly get the words out.

He nodded and loped off around behind his house to the path that would take him to the road that led to Waterloo— taking Charity's heart with him.

Chapter Twenty-Three

The early morning clamor of Kansas City made Brandon's head swim. After debarking at the train depot, he ambled down the street, reins in hand, taking in the bigness of the town while he looked for a modest hotel in which to register.

He'd made the ride to Waterloo with no problems, but with only seven minutes to spare before the train was scheduled to pull out. Once he bought his ticket and loaded his horse into a stock car, he'd hurried to the passenger car and took a seat just as the train blew its whistle, then lurched forward.

Crowds of cowboys, wagons, and stock all jockeyed for space on the road. Tall brick buildings, four and five stories high, lined the street for as far as he could see. Some looked as large as a whole city block. There were bookstores, general stores, fine-furniture establishments, and eateries galore. Some with white awnings, others red striped—some shading small tables and chairs. He stopped in front of a clothing store that would make Berta May green with envy, with hats, bolts of fabric, and knickknacks crammed in the window.

A steer came out of nowhere from behind and jostled his shoulder, forcing him to step back.

"Out of the way," the drover called crankily, and spit a stream of tobacco juice into the dirt-packed street.

Brandon smiled and looked around. That man wouldn't dim his spirits in the least. Nothing could now since his talk with Charity and the chance to explain himself. Thank God she'd come around to his way of thinking. The sensation of her in his arms was just about the best feeling in the world. Life was too short to stay rooted in one place year after year. There were places to discover. Might as well start right here in Kansas City.

MABLE BROWN'S INN AND ESTABLISHMENT. He read the sign positioned high on a blue-and-brown clapboard building.

"Just the kind of place I'm looking for," he said, knowing that the ratty-appearing hotel couldn't charge more than a dollar or two a night. A sign shaped like an arrow was tacked on the side of the building and pointed down the alley. It read: MABLE BROWN'S STABLE.

He nodded, pleased with himself on the good find. Right in the middle of everything. Couldn't be more convenient if it tried. After hitching his horse to the rail, he brushed the cinder and ash from his shirtsleeves and pants, then kicked the dirt from his boots against the well-worn boardwalk. He pushed open the door at the same time as he removed his hat. A couple of men talking in the lobby paid him no mind. A girl behind the counter looked up.

"May I help ya, sir?" She gazed at him expectantly. Her dress, ragged around the cuffs and collar, looked as if it could use a good scrub.

"Yes, I'd like a room for a couple of nights." He'd start with that and see how it went.

Her eyes brightened. A toothy smile broke out on her thin face, as if she'd expected him to turn on his heel after viewing the rundown interior of the lobby.

"Then you've come t'the right place. I have several rooms left, which is unusual for a Saturday night." She turned a large ledger around and handed him a pen. "Just sign here." She pointed to the middle of the page. "Beneath th'last name entered."

Sure, sure, Brandon thought. He reached in his pocket to pay her.

"That'll be eight dollars."

His hand froze inside his pocket, the leather pouch where he kept his money in his palm.

"Eight dollars for two nights? Isn't that a mite steep?"

She pulled back, as if surprised. "Why, no, sir. We're the most reasonable place in Kansas City." Her brow arched. "Well, one of 'em. There's a washroom at the end of the hall, an outhouse around back, and a simple breakfast comes with the price of the room. Now, do you have a horse you want to stable?"

The men standing in the lobby behind him stomped up the narrow staircase, glancing down at him for one brief second. They looked none too prosperous.

"Yes."

She bobbed with excitement. "Fine! That'll be a dollar more each day."

A bit grudgingly, Brandon fished out two five-dollar gold coins. *Ten dollars for this place?* Oh well, he'd make the best of it. Cattlemen's popped into his mind, and the bridal suite he'd looked into reserving for the wedding night. The spacious room had a large four-poster bed made of bird's-eye maple, and a nice view out back. It was expensive at three dollars and fifty cents a night, but that included a bottle of champagne, a soaking tub, breakfast in bed the next day—he hoped it wouldn't be Lenore Saffelberg serving—and a handmade pillow keepsake.

A smile teased his lips as he thought of Charity enjoying all those comforts…

The clerk cleared her throat. She looked at his hand. "The money, sir?"

He handed over his hard-earned pay, and looked around while she reached for a key in the slots behind her head. "Here ya go. The front door is locked at twelve o'clock, but if you're out late, just knock loudly and the cook that sleeps next to the kitchen will hear you and unlock the door."

"Thank you." He pocketed the key. "Is anyone around back?"

"No, sir. Da stable is self-serve."

Of course it is. He took out the letter. "Do you know where South Fillmore Street is?"

"Oh yes, sir! You just follow the street out front till you come to Blackstone. Turn left, follow to the end." She squinted again at the address. "On Stag Lane, go right, and that will run into Fillmore. I'd guess the address you're looking for will be on the right, but I'm not sure."

He smiled. "Thank you, miss. You've been very helpful."

That brought a bright, toothy smile aimed straight at him. "Oh, I almost forgot." She reached under the counter. "Here's a voucher for a half-price dinner at Henry's, just down the street about half a block. Pepper steak or gravy-covered pork chops are their specialties."

The thought of a good steak brought moisture to his mouth.

When he left the lobby, the blur of goings-on out on the street didn't feel quite so exciting anymore. Most pedestrians kept their heads down to watch where they set their feet, and the ones who did look up kept their gazes trained far away, proficient in avoiding any eye contact. God forbid they smiled and said hello.

Brandon gathered up his horse and proceeded around back. He'd give the gelding a nice rubdown after the long and fast gallop to Waterloo and the train ride, then follow it up with a generous portion of oats. Entering the quiet, shedlike barn, he found all six stalls empty. Plain dirt covered the stall floors, bare of any straw bedding, and after a quick search, he found only a small portion of dusty hay. No grain, no grooming tools. He shook his head in disgust. He should have checked this out before paying for two days.

Resigned, he unsaddled and stored his tack in a small room. With the towel from his saddlebag, he went over his horse's coat with a firm hand. Grasping the hay, he did his best to divest it of dust. It wouldn't do to have his horse up and colic on him.

Finished, he brushed the grime from his hands and clothes. As he listened to the munch of his horse eating, a pinch of hunger burned deep in his belly. Excitement once again zinged along Brandon's backbone. On Monday, he'd be reunited with the man who had been a father figure in his mind for years. A rush of pride warmed him when he pictured Timberlake's face from so many years ago.

Was this his destiny? To follow in Timberlake's footsteps? What better way than to work with him every day. He hadn't expected the renowned marshal to remember a sniveling boy grieving his parents, who had then shaken his small fist at the outlaw stretched out on the ground next to them. Had it been coincidence that brought the lawman along the road at the exact time of the robbery? Brandon had always wondered about that. Perhaps it was because he was meant to come to Missouri and make a name for himself. One equal to or greater than Timberlake himself.

Remembering the voucher in his pocket, he gathered his saddlebags and went in search of Henry's.

Chapter Twenty-Four

There days had passed since Brandon left Y Knot, and Luke wished there was something he could do to cheer up Charity. The expression on her face when she thought no one was looking was enough to make even him cry. Word had leaked out to the rest of the family—thought to have come from Jack—that Brandon had gone to Missouri to see about a deputy marshal's job. The family was hurt and confused.

"How could he even think of doing such a thing at a time like this?" Faith had asked last night over supper. She'd tried to hide her disquiet, but it proved difficult. "They just set the date, for heaven's sake. I can't say I'm not disappointed in him." He hadn't had an answer for her.

Fox Dancing was now up and getting around, although still weak. Luke was catching on to her signs and some of the words. They brought a lightness to his heart, although he never let on around Flood. He wished there was something he could say to his pa, but what? There was a hurt so big there, resurrected by the appearance of Fox Dancing, that Luke didn't know if they'd ever get back to normal. With Charity, and Fox Dancing, and Flood and his mother, the Heart of the Mountains felt under siege.

The sound of horses arriving brought Luke out of his barn, where he'd been lamenting the state of affairs as he cleaned out a stall. Chance rode up, along with Tobit Preece.

"Chance. Tobit. What brings you out our way?"

Chance dismounted, followed by Isaiah Preece's grandson. He'd met the young farmer a few times over the last two months.

"I heard about the lumpy jaw, Luke," Chance said. "That's unfortunate. How many infected animals you got?"

"Only about nine, so far. But we're still finding 'em."

"I'm watching my cattle, but I haven't seen any sign, and that's a huge relief. With a small herd like I have, every head counts."

"Every head counts in a large herd too."

Chance nodded. He tipped his hat back, taking stock of the place. A surge of pride in his homestead flowed through Luke.

"You're right," Chance agreed. "But lumpy jaw's not why I rode out. Seems we had a visitor to our new chicken coop last night."

Luke leaned back on the fence and propped his boot on the bottom rail. When he glanced toward the house, he noticed Fox Dancing watching from the front window. Faith liked her well enough, and little Dawn was totally smitten. His daughter was learning Cheyenne faster than she had English.

That worried him. He was sensitive to Flood, and what he was going through. His ma came out almost every evening. Luke would sit and watch this magical thing between her and Fox Dancing as his mother renewed her knowledge of the language amid laughter and, once in a while, tears. He couldn't help but wonder if she'd ever asked Fox Dancing about his real father. But Flood, that was a different story. He hadn't been out once.

"Oh?" he said to Chance. "Coyote or fox?"

"Neither. The critter unlatched the gate and caught Evie's favorite laying hen. On the way out, they hooked the latch, trying to make it appear as if nothing had happened. The dog didn't hear them and there wasn't a track to be found."

Luke dropped his gaze to where his hand still gripped the hayfork. "You sure? Are you saying a person came out to your place and stole your chicken? Couldn't the hen have found a way out, a mole hole you missed or a portion where the wire isn't tight to the earth? If she did, she'd have been caught by some animal and carried off."

"Not likely. That coop is brand new. And I built it strong and made sure there was no getting in or getting out without unlatching the gate. What has me spooked is the lack of tracks of any kind. More like an Indian than a white man."

Luke straightened. Here was the real reason for the visit. Any mention of an Indian, even an injured young girl, put people on edge. No one wanted trouble with the natives. The bloody conflicts hadn't been that long ago—and prejudice still ran strong.

Chance raised a palm. "Hold on, Luke. You're jumping to conclusions before I even finish what I rode out here to say. I may have wrote the hen off to circumstance, as you say, but Tobit had the same thing happen out at his place two days before. I know you have a guest, and also that she's hurt, ruling her out as suspect. So just stop drilling me with that accusatory glower."

Tobit stood back and let Chance do the talking. Luke had a history with Chance—the cowhand used to work for them and was more like a brother than a neighbor. But he hardly knew Tobit. He wondered if Chance's neighbor knew his history and the fact that he was a half-breed. Probably did. Information like that was just too good to keep quiet.

The door opened and Faith came a few steps out of the house, a dish towel in her hands. "Hi, boys," she called and waved. "Would you like a slice of chocolate cake? It's still warm."

A sentimental smile curled Chance's lips. "No, thank you, Faith. We're just out here for a minute. But that sure sounds good."

She tipped her head and Luke knew what was coming. He pushed back a stab of jealousy.

"You sure? When was the last time you had chocolate cake?" she asked.

Chance looked at Tobit.

"Been about six months for me," Tobit said to Chance.

"I had some last week, Miss Faith, but it's been half a year for Tobit here. Maybe we can stay a few extra minutes and partake."

Her face lit up like the sun and Luke couldn't fault her for being neighborly.

"Wonderful. When you're finished with your business, come on in."

Fox Dancing watched from the window as her brother and two other white men approached the front door. A pain in her upper arm pulsated, and she cupped her bandaged wound with her other hand. By the look on Luk's face, he wasn't pleased with the news the men had brought. When Dawn tugged on her hand, Fox Dancing looked down and smiled.

This girl child, with hair the color of the sun's shimmering rays, had stolen her heart. She felt no suspicion or fear from her. Just curiosity and love.

The door opened. The men stepped in and removed their hats, something she was getting used to seeing. Never one to run and hide away, she lifted her chin and gave them a long, solemn look. She was not afraid, even in her weakened state. She was safe in this house.

"Oh," the first man said when he noticed her.

Luk cleared his throat, then gave her a small smile. "How's the arm this morning, Fox Dancing?" He pointed to the bandage, as he did often.

She nodded. "Good." At her word, Dawn grasped the hand of her uninjured arm and dragged her forward.

The newcomers looked between themselves.

"Hey, Dawn," the taller of the two said. He put his arms out and the child hurried to him. He bundled her into a hug and she kissed his cheek.

"Make yourselves comfortable," Faith called from the kitchen. "I'll be right there."

The three men left their hats on the rack by the door and sat at the table. Faith carried in a tray and set a generous portion of the light chocolate confection before each man, and a cup of coffee. One small slice she put next to Luk, then pulled a chair over. Dawn climbed up and sat on her knees. "The coffee's just perked," Faith said. "I have cream and sugar too, if you'd like."

"Yes, ma'am," both guests said.

"I'll be right back."

Fox Dancing's mouth watered as she remembered the slice she'd consumed a few minutes before the riders appeared. It was soft and warm, and it tickled the insides of her mouth with what felt like a smile. She enjoyed the treat, as Faith had called it.

Her brother took a big bite and chewed, his eyes closing in pleasure.

"So, Luke," one of the men said while eating, "getting back to the reason for our visit. We wanted to warn you. So you'd keep your eyes open."

"What's this about?" Faith asked as she put a small pitcher of cream and the sugar in the center of the table. Her brows pulled down as she gave a glass of milk to Dawn and ruffled her daughter's hair. "You eat slowly. This is your second piece." She looked to the man who was doing all the talking. "Warn us about what, Chance?"

"Just that we have reason to believe there may be Indians in the area, sneaking around. Tobit and I had some fowl stolen out of their pens in the last few days."

Luk harrumphed.

The men kept their gazes trained away from her, but Fox Dancing still felt the unsaid accusation that hung in the air. She'd not drop her guard for even a second. Not all whites would be as welcoming as her brother and his family.

Chapter Twenty-Five

The soggy meat and potatoes Henry's had offered as their Saturday night special sat in Brandon's stomach like a bucket of lead nails. He stretched out on the small bed and tried to get comfortable. The meal had been atrocious. Not only did it keep coming back up, coating his mouth with an oily taste, but it had lightened his travel expense money by almost two dollars—even at half price.

He closed his eyes for a moment and thought about the tasty roast beef dinner at the barn party last Saturday night. The meat, so tender you could cut it with your fork, and side dishes almost made him whimper in need. The plentiful, mouthwatering desserts brought a deep longing. Now, *that* was a meal.

With the window wide open, the noise from the street sounded like it was right in the room. The tinny piano music from two doors down pounded out the same four songs per half hour. Loud laughter, as well as guns discharging every so often, had his nerves strung tight.

Brandon had tried closing the window, but the room was stifling. He'd stripped to his undershirt and long johns, but by now they were wet with sweat and stuck to his body like a second skin.

Who knew Kansas City would be so doggone hot and humid? When dust rained down into his face, Brandon glanced up at the ceiling beam that ran the length of the room to see a small mouse scampering across.

Agitated, he blew the particles from his face and stood, crossing to the dresser on the opposite side of the room. He poured a glass of water from the dented metal pitcher. Just as he raised it to his lips, a large bug floated in front of his face, feet up.

Disgusted, he slammed the glass down, sloshing water everywhere. Determined to get out of there, he pulled on his shirt, followed by his pants and boots. He needed some air before he suffocated. He'd tack his horse and ride to the outskirts, where he could get a little peace and quiet. Thinking of his bedroll on the back of his saddle, he was tempted to throw it on the ground and get a good night's rest under the stars.

With his Colt .45 strapped on and his sheriff's star in plain sight, he hefted his saddlebags and exited his room. The air cooled a mite as he descended the stairs, but he still missed the cool Montana nights.

It was nine o'clock. The lobby was empty. He stepped onto the street, into the throng of men and some women, most the not-so-genteel type. When a gun discharged— again—making him flinch, he wondered where the sheriff was, or Timberlake, or someone. He wasn't going to get involved.

Surprised at the indifference he felt toward the town, he started down the alley to the stable. He couldn't even muster the enthusiasm to see some sights, have a drink in the saloon, or talk to anyone. He supposed he'd feel different if Charity were here with him, but he'd never know now.

He had his horse saddled within minutes. Walking through the alley, he entered the main street, eager to get some space around him. Glancing up, he tried to gauge the stars, but the tall buildings all around made it impossible to see much, only a small patch of dark sky covered with wispy clouds. The directions the lobby clerk had given him popped into his mind, so Brandon decided to go in that direction, then continue until he hit some peace and quiet. He kept to the middle of the street. Getting killed now by some drunk, outlaw, or stray bullet would be a bitter pill when he had such a prize waiting at the end of the month.

His heart surged.

Charity.

Only a few days apart, and it felt like a year. The time they'd had at his house, with her sitting on his lap, had been just about the best day of his life. He'd been so discouraged that morning, having to leave without resolving their differences. It was a welcome sight when she rode up. What was she doing tonight? How were things progressing with Luke's Cheyenne sister?

"Hey, mister," a man called from the edge of the boardwalk. He swayed dangerously to one side, but caught the lamp pole just in time and stayed on his feet. "You got two bits to spare?"

Brandon took in his raggedy appearance. "Nope. Sure don't." *And if I did, I wouldn't give it to you.*

"Have a heart. I haven't eaten for days."

Yeah, right.

When Brandon rode past, the man's pleasant smile disappeared and he spat out few choice words, which Brandon was happy to ignore.

Kansas City was not what he'd expected. But he wasn't being fair. He had to give it time.

He removed his hat and swiped his hand across his wet brow, then replaced it with a tug. What a time to come to town. When he'd gone down to the lobby for a fresh towel, the gal had said they were having a heat wave, but that they usually didn't last long, just a week or two. He ignored the sweat running down his temples as he rode and took stock of the Kansas City nightlife.

After making several turns, he came to Fillmore Street. Reading the addresses was difficult in the darkness, but some addresses were close enough to lampposts that he was able to make them out. Timberlake's office must be around here somewhere. The street was an odd mix of houses, businesses, and open lots. He had the entire day tomorrow to kill, before reporting to the marshal's office on Monday.

He tried to dredge up an increment of the excitement he'd felt on the train ride southeast—remembering his joy over Charity's visit to see him off.

She'd been thinking of him, as usual, and didn't want him to fret. Knowing him so well, she'd acknowledged he'd mull over their situation until he beat it dead and then some. She'd wanted to put his mind at ease. And she had, at least for a few days.

Now…he wasn't quite sure. The farther he got away from Y Knot, and as the days passed, perhaps he'd been hasty to think he was still on firm ground with Charity.

He took a deep breath, expecting the freshness of the Montana air, but his chest clenched and he coughed. Coal dust was everywhere, a result of all the factories. He pulled up, looking at the buildings around him.

At least come Monday, he'd know the general vicinity where he needed to be. In the light of day he'd be able to find the marshal's office.

With a satisfied nod, and the noise of the downtown growing farther behind him, he headed to the outskirts, where he'd be able to get a breath of clean air and enjoy the sound of the crickets. Once he met Timberlake, he was sure all the enthusiasm he'd felt when he'd first written to the lawman would return. This was a person who linked him with his parents, the only family he had. At that thought, all the long Sunday night dinners he'd enjoyed at the McCutcheon ranch popped into his head. The back of his eyes stung, but he pushed the sentiment away.

The image of his parents lying dead on the cold November ground almost stole his breath. At the time it happened, Timberlake was a young man, probably younger than his own twenty-five years, and yet he'd taken the time to comfort a small boy he hadn't even known. Brandon remembered crying in his arms for a good long time.

The man had loaded his parents' bodies, along with the outlaw's, into the back of the buckboard and turned the conveyance around, then led the horses back to town. He'd let Brandon ride behind him on the horse. Brandon could still remember the feel of his fisted hands gripping the young lawman's shirt. He'd cried again when Timberlake had left him with several ladies at the town church. And that had begun his life of moving from household to household until he was twelve, when he'd snuck away in the night. But before that, Timberlake would visit from time to time, say hello, take him for a meal. Brandon had lived for those moments.

Monday would be like that, just like old times, wouldn't it? He looked up at the stars, finally far enough from town to be able to make out the Big Dipper.

Charity loved looking at the stars...

Chapter Twenty-Six

Tired of moping around, Charity had decided enough was enough. She went out to the back corral to catch her palomino mare. She needed to get her emotions in check. Tomorrow would mark two weeks since she and Brandon had returned to Y Knot, filled with exciting plans for their future.

How had things gone so wrong? It was hard to know. Getting away from the house might help. The tension between her parents wasn't getting any better, and it had her more than worried. Her father was getting home late almost every night, claiming all sorts of chores as crazy excuses.

Charity's mare lifted her head when her mistress approached. Haltering her, Charity led her into the barn, and quickly tacked her up. She wanted to get over to Luke's and spend some time with Fox Dancing. Plus, she intended to share her concerns about their parents with Luke.

A noise caught her attention.

She turned to find Francis hanging back by the barn doors, a rope coiled in his hands and uncertainty written on his face. He'd been scarce since her visit to the bunkhouse, and this was the first time they'd come face-to-face.

"I could've got your horse for you, Miss Charity."

His contrite tone tugged at her. She wasn't mad at him. She just wanted things to be back to normal. "Thanks, Francis. I enjoy saddling her, but that was a nice thought. How've you been?"

When he came forward a few steps, she did the same, and they met in the middle of the barn.

"All right, I guess. Most of the work doctoring the cattle is done, unless we find more infected beef."

His voice was so much deeper than she remembered. He'd filled out. His sinewy arms were now thick, and his chest wide. He stood a full head and a half taller than her. He hadn't shaved today, and the beginnings of a dark shadow covered his jaw.

Francis had bloomed and she hadn't noticed.

"We still got to keep them separate, though," he said. "Until they can't spread their infected saliva on the ground as they graze. You know, so the rest of the stock don't pick it up."

"Good, good," she said, nodding. She wanted to keep the conversation going, so they could get back onto solid ground. She'd missed Francis's gentle teasing and friendly smiles. "If we stay to the twelve head we have quarantined, we're getting off easy, at least in my mind. Are Smokey and Ike doing most of the doctoring?"

He nodded, then, for several long seconds, glanced down the barn aisle to where her horse was tied. "Miss Charity, there's something I'd like to say, and if I don't do it now, I may not get another chance. I haven't gotten much sleep these past few nights, and I'm sure you know why."

She could nod yes, but that might stop him, so instead she just looked at him.

"Those things I said about Brandon and Miss Aubrey weren't true. When I came into the saloon, they was talkin', but not in any lovey-dovey secret kind of way like I led you to believe. I think Abe had just introduced 'em. I made that whole story up."

Her heart warmed. The color in his face had deepened to an overripe strawberry, and he looked cute.

"I see."

"I hope I didn't cause no trouble between the two of you."

She reached out and touched his arm. "No, you didn't. But I appreciate you straightening it out for me."

"I thought maybe that was why Brandon decided to take that job in Kansas City. You told him what I said and the two of you got back to fightin'."

At the mention of Brandon's name, she blinked and looked away. She'd been doing so well, enjoying the time spent with her horse, with big plans not to think of him today or wonder what he was doing.

"Charity, I'm sorry." It was a husky plea. "I don't know what got into me."

"No, it wasn't you." *And he hasn't taken the job yet. If my prayers carry any weight at all, he won't.* If she tried to explain that Brandon was just *thinking* about the job, that it wasn't set in stone, Francis would never believe her. Especially if the scuttlebutt around the bunkhouse was that Brandon had already gone. She didn't have the energy to try to straighten it out. "I never mentioned anything to Brandon about what you said, so his leaving had nothing to do with you, Francis."

Francis nodded, but his eyes said he didn't believe her for a minute.

"That's the truth. I'm not making it up to make you feel better."

The sound of voices from outside made him pull up straight.

"I hope that's true, Miss Charity. I want you to know I hope he comes back. And that the two of you get married, just like you planned. I do. Because I know that's the only thing that will make you happy."

She stepped forward and wrapped him in a hug, even though he remained stiff as a fencepost. Finally, he put his arms around her. "Thank you. But you have to promise me that if that doesn't happen, you won't think it has anything to do with you—because it won't. Nothing at all."

She felt him nod, and she stepped away. "Good. I'm glad that's all cleared up."

"So am I," he said sheepishly.

"Now, will you please tell my parents when you see them that I'm riding over to Luke and Faith's? I want to spend some time with Fox Dancing, get to know her. It's about time I gave her a proper welcome to the family." She strode over and gathered her horse's reins. Passing Francis as she exited the barn, she called over her shoulder. "No more long nights lying awake in bed, you hear!"

When he chuckled, she wondered if she could do the same. She wished sleep were as easy as that, but it wasn't the case. She wouldn't sleep a wink until Brandon was back for good. If he returned at all.

Oh, it was good to be outside of the dwelling. Fox Dancing lifted her face to the sun, absorbing its warmth and energy.

She was overjoyed when Luk said they had found her horse. Now, filled with energy, and with an arm that barely hurt, she was happier than she'd felt in months. She walked beside her older brother, brimming with pride.

Inside the barn, Luk stopped and looked over the side of a stall. "Here she is. She had a few scrapes, but I've treated them and I'm sure she'll heal nicely."

When she looked in, her horse picked up her head from her feed and came to the gate, bumping it with her chest. Her ears flicked back and forth, and Fox Dancing was sure she was unhappy about being kept in the small, dark enclosure. It took her a minute to figure out the gate latch, then she opened the stall and went inside.

She put her arm around her mare's neck and a surge of homesickness washed through her. How was grandfather? Was his strength holding out? He was eager to put this life behind him and move on to better hunting grounds. What about her father and mothers, and also Painted Bear Stone? Did they miss her? What had they thought when she hadn't appeared from the tepee for the morning meal? She rubbed her face against the warm coat, almost forgetting her brother stood very close.

"Fox Dancing? Are you all right?"

She jerked, surprised to feel a drop of moisture in her eye. She quickly blinked it away and turned to him.

"Are you sad?" he asked in his deep, worried voice.

She shook her head, and then smiled. "No. Happy." Happy was a word Dawn had taught her, and it was coming in very handy. "Happy found white brother."

And she was. But she did miss her family more than she had anticipated she would when she began planning how to escape her marriage to Painted Bear Stone. The knowledge that he would be asking for her soon had kept her awake at night for the past months. He'd gone from boy to young warrior, and his company made her anxious. Made her nerves tingle and her blood run hot. The unsettled feeling confused her. He was overbearing, especially when he thought he had her full attention, flashing his charming smile as if he were the only male in their village. Now, he'd have to choose another bride from the other girls who had come of age this year. Any of them would eagerly take her place.

Luk looked pleased. With a fisted hand, he thumped his chest twice, and then pointed to her. "I'm happy you found me too."

"Pa!"

Dawn dashed into the barn, her dress billowing behind her. With a snort, Fox Dancing's mare twirled away, frightened, and presented her hip. The child skidded to a halt at her father's feet.

"Hey there, honey." Luke swung her up into his arms. "What's so urgent?"

She held out a handful of greens. "For Penlupee Fowers."

The child's eyes sparkled with happiness, reminding Fox Dancing of the little children she'd left behind. Even with their hardships and hungry bellies, they found things to smile about.

Luk tickled his daughter under her chin, making her giggle. "Did Ma give you that to feed her favorite cow?"

Dawn nodded.

"Well, let's go. Follow us, Fox Dancing. We've failed to introduce you to a very special part of our family. She's around this way, outside at the back of the barn."

"Luke." They turned when Faith called from the house. "Charity's coming up the hill. Her and two other riders."

Luk set Dawn down. "You go ahead, sweetie. Just stay on this side of the fence. Come back as soon as you've fed Penelope." She nodded again, and darted off. Luk gestured for Fox Dancing to follow. "Let's go see who's coming for a visit."

When Luke recognized Jack Jones and Sheriff Huxley riding in with Charity, he cursed himself. He'd expected the riders to be Smokey or Roady, or another hand from the ranch, not Brandon's deputy and the sheriff of Pine Grove. He stopped, and Fox Dancing did too. She looked trustingly into his eyes.

"Go inside," he said, and pointed.

Faith was watching them from the door. Her brows were pulled down and she seemed to pick up on what he was thinking. Why go looking for trouble?

Fox Dancing's gaze cut to Charity and the men. She nodded. Even at her age, she must know the ways of the white man and all the suffering they'd caused over the years.

When the women disappeared behind the closed door, Luke turned to greet the new arrivals. "Charity," he said as she dismounted. "Jack. Huxley."

Charity gestured to the men, who remained on their horses. "I ran into Jack and Sheriff Huxley on their way out to the ranch looking for you. When they learned I was on my way over here, they decided to come along." Her brow arched when their gazes locked.

He felt her anxiety. What were these men about? When she stepped close to his side, he wondered all the more.

"What can I do for you, Jack? Sheriff?"

The old man shifted in his saddle. "Word got to Pine Grove that you have an Indian staying at your place," he said loudly. "And a wounded one at that. You know we had us some trouble recently. Just wanted to have a word with her, if I could. Ask her a few questions. See if she saw anything suspicious."

"An Indian *girl*. And no, you can't."

"Luke," Jack said, his lips forming an agitated, flat line. "It'll only take one minute. Then we'll be out of your hair."

"She's not feeling up to it," Luke lied. He'd do anything to shield his own flesh and blood, especially after her valiant effort to find him. Making that dangerous trip all by herself, even being so young, had touched him. He'd not give her up to them—ever.

"We just saw her go inside," Jack said. "She's up and walking, at least. I'm sure she can answer Huxley's questions. If not, we may get to thinking you're hidin' somethin'."

Luke took a step toward them, and he felt Charity's hand on his arm.

"This is her first time out of the house. She's still weak. But that's beside the point. I don't want you to talk to her. What in the world could you gain from that?"

"I'm under the impression she was traveling through our country right around the time that calf that Brandon helped investigate was slaughtered. And that's about the same time Drake and his friend were killed."

Luke tamped back his temper.

"You told Brandon those two miners killed each other. Got into some disagreement and ended up dead. Now, you're changing your story because an Indian may have come within a few miles of their place?"

Huxley took off his hat with a shaky hand and wiped his brow. "I just feel there's more to the story now. You know how investigating goes."

"Sure I do. Don't matter about evidence, just the color of the skin. Now, unless you came out for anything else, we're done talking."

Chapter Twenty-Seven

The row of two-story homes, most having seen better days, ran the length of the road, interspersed with businesses. Brandon dismounted, nerves pulled tight. It still amazed him how so many people could be crammed into one small area.

He slipped his reins into a ring at the top of a waist-high black metal post and stretched his aching back. The ground might have been hard the last two nights, but the air, temperature, and sights were well worth sleeping out. He'd yet to eat, but planned to remedy that just as soon as he'd met with Timberlake.

Still unable to spot the correct address, Brandon climbed the stairs of the nearest house and knocked on the door. A well-turned-out young woman answered. Her brows lifted after she looked him up and down. "The ice needs to be taken to the door 'round back," she stated flatly. "I don't know how many times we have to tell you people that."

Brandon clenched his jaw. "I'm not a deliveryman, miss. Was wondering if you could tell me where Marshal Timberlake's office is."

Her lip curled up. "Oh, I'm sorry to mistake you."

"No harm done."

She pointed across the street.

"His office is down that alley next to the blue house. It's the lean-to. You'll find it easily."

What? A lean-to in an alley? He hadn't had big expectations, but a lean-to in an alley was far from it. "Thank you."

When she closed the door, Brandon turned and retrieved his horse. He didn't mount, just walked across the road and down the alley. Just like she'd promised, a rickety lean-to butted up next to a blue house. All was quiet, and he wondered if Timberlake was in the house sleeping. Must be that this was his house, and the shanty out back was his office. Anything but pleased, he secured his horse out front, pushed open the door of the lean-to, and stopped.

The place looked as if it hadn't seen a broom for years. Paper and junk littered the place and the desk was piled high. Brandon wondered how the man found anything. *Paperwork and cleanliness don't make a lawman. Timberlake was credited with breaking up the Younger gang. That means more than housekeeping.* There wasn't an empty chair, even if he did want to sit down.

Without warning, the door swung open. The man who came in wasn't old enough to be James Timberlake. He pulled up, surprised.

"Who're you?"

He wore guns, a vest, and a star. He must be a deputy.

"Brandon Crawford, sheriff of Y Knot, Montana."

The man hung his hat and went behind the desk. He started pushing papers around as if looking for something.

"You're a long ways from home, Sheriff," he said, looking up briefly. "What brings you out our way?"

They weren't expecting him? Anger pricked Brandon's mind. "James Timberlake. He here?"

As if exasperated, the deputy scraped the junk off the chair and it clattered to the floor. He sat down. "Feel free to do the same," he said, and pointed to a chair.

"No, thanks. Just need to see the marshal. Is he inside?"

"Inside?"

"His house."

Seemed to take a few seconds for the deputy to pick up on his meaning, and then he barked out a laugh.

"He don't own no fancy house like that, just an old farm eight miles out of town. If you want to ride out there, I'm sure you'll find him and his missus—probably working the fields."

Farming! Brandon struggled to wrap his head around the deputy's statement.

"He never mentioned me, or that I'd be arriving today?"

An eight-mile ride out of town sounded as appealing as a poke in the eye with a sharp stick. Not after hanging around all day yesterday, fighting the crowds, breathing dank, heavy air that burned one's lungs, and feeling as comfortable as a fish in sand. "To discuss the deputy job?"

The deputy stood, shaking his head. "Damn the old codger. He talks about hiring a few new deputies about every other day. Never has as long as I've been here, and that's a good six years." He made a face. "I think it's the opium eating away at his brain."

Several moments passed as the meaning of the deputy's words sank in. Timberlake wasn't the man he remembered as a boy—far from it, it seemed.

Disappointment ripped through him, but turned into anger almost immediately. Not at Timberlake, but at himself. For not seeing what he had right in front of his face. How stupid could he be, chasing a dream and throwing away all that he held dear? No, he'd not ride a foot farther to talk with a man he hadn't known for years. He didn't want to stay in this cramped city where the buildings blocked out the stars, and where some bum waited to knock you on your head and steal you blind. He could never bring Charity here. She belonged in the high mountains of Montana with her family.

Was he too late? Charity was everything to him. Much more than a remembered feeling about his parents. As much as it had haunted him, it was the past. Where he'd now let it die, while he moved on with his life. He prayed to God Charity would still have him. He wouldn't blame her in the least if she told him to go to the devil. How fast could he make it home?

"You gonna go out and see him? I'm sure he'd like to at least talk to you, since you've come so far."

Brandon shook his head. "No. I'll not waste any more of my time." *Charity.* "If Timberlake happens to remember about me and ask, just tell him Brandon Crawford went back to the clean air of Montana where he belongs."

He realized with satisfaction that he'd come to that decision almost as soon as he'd stepped off the train, he'd just been too mixed up to see it.

"I can see you're plenty put out, Crawford, and I don't blame you. Timberlake means well, and gets the job done when needed. He just has a bit of a problem focusing on what his objective should be each given day."

Brandon turned on his heel and made for his horse. All his belongings were packed and with him. That was one plus, that he didn't have to go back to the inn. He'd head straight to the station and hope there was an early train leaving west this morning. West, Y Knot, home…*and* Charity.

Now that he'd finally come to terms with his unsettled past, he couldn't return fast enough to his future. He just hoped that, after all his shenanigans, he still had one.

Chapter Twenty-Eight

Luke slid the chute gate open and signaled for Charity and Colton to push the next heifer into the narrow slot. Only a few more head to go and they'd be finished for the day. Most of the beef had made good progress since they'd undergone the iodine treatments.

"Bring in the short one, Colton, the one behind you," he called. "She's quick, though, so be ready."

"Sure thing, Pa," he called back. That boy loved ranching. He'd taken to it like a natural, and Luke couldn't be prouder of him if he tried. The boy was still mounted on Firefly, the old mare Luke had given him on a cattle drive three years ago. As much as Colton loved the old horse, he was ready and capable enough for a new mount. Maybe not War Bonnet yet, but Luke would make sure the spirited gelding was good and broke before he handed the horse over.

When the heifer darted in, Luke jammed the gate into place behind her hips and stood back, wiping his gloved hands down his legs. She rattled the wood as she banged around, looking for a way out. Not finding one, she quieted.

Charity climbed directly from the back of her horse onto the fence, and down the other side. She went to the front of the chute with Smokey, Roady, and Pedro. Flood stood behind the group with his back to a pine, watching.

"Give me a second," Charity said. She scooped a glob of molasses onto a clean wooden tongue depressor, large enough for the bovine, and got into place.

Luke was keenly aware of Fox Dancing's gaze as she watched them work from the bare back of her Appaloosa mare outside of the corral. Whatever they were doing, she was never far from his side—and it warmed him. Amazing how he'd actually found part of his heritage, or how it found him. Considerate of Flood's feelings, whatever they were at this point, he'd kept his Cheyenne sister away from the ranch house for as long as he could. But the work wouldn't wait any longer. There were things to get done.

"Ready, Charity?" Smokey drawled. He stood beside the chute by the heifer's head. Pedro and Roady were positioned on top, ready to grab the nose and jaw to keep it open so Luke could peer inside. If they needed another dose of iodine, it would be done now. Doctoring an animal this size wasn't easily accomplished. The molasses distracted the animal, while making it smack its mouth.

Charity held the long tool with the gooey, dark glob in front. "Ready!"

Smokey nodded. "Here goes." He dug his gloved thumb inside the heifer's mouth, into the gum, making her open just wide enough for Charity to slip in the sweetness. The moment the cow tasted the molasses, her tongue wagged out. Pedro and Roady both grasped her head and nose and pried her mouth open.

Luke squatted in front and peered in. "One more second, boys. Hold on, hold on. There! Good."

The cowboys let go and jumped down. The heifer, none the worse for it, kept smacking her mouth, enjoying the treat.

"She looks good." He pulled open the front gate, and the young cow bolted out and bucked a few times before Billy and Adam, Matthew's two sons, herded it toward the gate of the small pasture, where the rest of the recuperating animals grazed.

The day couldn't end fast enough for Luke. He had plans to take Faith and the children into Y Knot and to the Biscuit Barrel for pie, the family-oriented restaurant's Wednesday night special. Most of the McCutcheons made a habit of it, and practically filled the small restaurant if everyone showed. He'd been debating whether he would take Fox Dancing. She'd made a good recovery and had been up for several days, and riding the last few. But was taking her into town a wise move? He'd feel a whole lot better if Brandon were back.

Flood came forward. Luke hadn't seen his parents in the same place, at the same time, since the night of the party. Something had to be done.

"I say we call it a day," Flood said. "Get cleaned up for tonight. Won't hurt the few remaining steers to wait a day or two."

Luke was beat. He'd been up since four thirty. And Charity was putting on a good show, but he could tell the last few days had taken their toll. He didn't want to think about the outcome of Brandon's trip. He couldn't imagine this place without his sister. It wouldn't feel right. But if she had to make a choice, he felt pretty sure she'd go with Brandon.

"Sounds good to me. Gives a little time to get ready before Faith and Dawn start clamoring to get moving to the Biscuit Barrel. Who all is—"

Francis's shout came from the barn.

Luke turned, as did the other hands. When another shout went up, everyone started for the structure. Before they got there, Francis and another fellow, locked in an embrace, careened through the dark opening into the bright afternoon sunlight. They landed in the dirt with a thud.

The two young men rolled. Luke caught a glimpse of a shirtless Indian, dressed much like Fox Dancing. The youth and Francis were evenly matched—except for the wicked-looking knife the native gripped in his hand. Francis grappled with the arm holding the weapon, pushing the Indian's wrist back. Both men shook as they strained forward.

Luke held back Roady when he went to help. "Wait! You may get Francis killed."

Fox Dancing, appearing at his side, yelled angrily at the two, yet didn't try to stop them either. Her heated Cheyenne words drew no response.

The two rolled through the dirt, wrapped together like two sides of a clam. The warrior's long hair tangled behind him. Next to some bushes and the watering trough, the brave made a quick scramble, issued a loud war cry, and bolted, disappearing into the trees.

"Do you want me to go after him?" Roady asked, looking toward his horse tied at the hitching rail.

"No, let him go."

Fox Dancing moved to follow, but Luke grabbed her wrist, holding her back. She looked back and forth from the path the brave had taken to Luke, her eyes flashing with anger and something else, plainly torn about what to do. Another loud cry came from beyond the pasture. Only a horse could have gotten away that fast.

Francis climbed to his feet. "I found him hiding in the back stall," he said, dusting the dirt from his clothes. A line of blood ran from his split lip down his chin, and a raw, dirt-filled abrasion on his face looked painful. Hay and dirt clung to his hair.

"Didn't realize he was an Indian until I went into the stall to see what was going on."

Flood placed both hands on Francis's shoulders, taking stock of their youngest cowhand. "I'm glad you came through that." It would be a sad day if anything ever happened to Francis. After satisfying himself that Francis would be fine, his pa said, "Go have Lucky clean you up."

"What in blue blazes is going on out here?" Lucky stepped out onto the bunkhouse porch just as Francis approached. He gaped. "You been tangling with a broken-tailed badger? I hope the other guy looks worse than you."

Lucky glanced around as if expecting to see another man with a bruised and bloodied face. Even though his words were teasing, Lucky's brows pulled down and he limped forward to help Francis when he wobbled.

Francis stopped halfway across the barnyard. "Who was the Indian, anyway?" he asked, turning back to Luke and Fox Dancing. "Does anyone know?"

Roady whistled. "Not certain, but sure was a strong cuss, Francis." He gave a little chuckle. "You should have seen yourself, though. You're stronger than any of us thought."

This was a fine can of worms. How many more Cheyenne would Luke have showing up now that Fox Dancing had arrived? Was that Fox Dancing's brother, and so his too? A warm surge of curiosity tickled his mind. A completely new world had opened to him. By the look on Fox Dancing's face, and her desire to follow the Indian brave, it was a sure bet that she knew who he was.

Luke chanced a look at Flood and saw his father's shoulders slumped. He couldn't remember seeing that in all his years, and it troubled him more than he'd like to admit. The ranch house door opened, and his ma came out. She went about cutting flowers, unaware of being observed. Flood's gaze watched each step she took, a somberness enveloping him. Whatever threatened the family or the ranch, the man who'd raised him usually took any problem straight on and didn't look back. Luke's heritage was once again bringing tension down on everyone.

"Pa, can I speak with you for a moment?" he said quietly while Charity went into the barn to stable her horse, with Fox Dancing following slowly behind.

Flood gave him a quizzical expression. "Sure, son."

Luke gestured with his head and Flood followed, as if they were going over to the pasture's edge to look at the cattle.

Flood gazed out at the land, avoiding Luke's gaze. "What's on your mind?"

It had been a good long time since Luke had consulted his pa for advice. The last important talk he could remember was when he was having doubts about Faith and her inability to trust him, to tell him the truth. Flood had directed Luke to give her time to come around, not to push too hard. Luke wondered how hard he'd have to push today.

"I think you know."

Flood nodded slowly and removed his hat, running his large, work-worn hand through his hair. "Yep, I suppose I do."

He turned and looked into Luke's eyes. Lines in his pa's face had deepened over the year, and the gray hair at his temples and salted through his still-thick brown hair had multiplied. "Are you thinking about going to meet your real pa?"

Surprised, Luke stepped back. He'd been so wrapped up in the relationship between his parents, he hadn't had a chance to consider his father's feelings toward him. He hadn't realized that besides worrying about his wife, Flood might be lamenting the loss of his son's love.

"I'd be a liar if I said the idea hadn't crossed my mind. And maybe I will someday. But not now. Discovering I have another sister, and actually meeting her, is enough change for me. My main concerns now, and always, are Faith and my family, and of course you and Ma. You're my father. There's no confusion in my heart over that fact."

For the first time ever, Luke noted the color as it came up in Flood's face.

"You know, you're free to go anytime you want. I can understand how you'd like to meet him face-to-face. That you'd have questions. That's understandable of any fellow. We'll watch over Faith and the young'uns."

Luke cut his gaze away. He couldn't look another moment upon the desperation in the man who'd raised him, loved him, and stood up for him when townsfolk called him a half-breed. It ripped his gut more than a bullet would. Flood was the most courageous man he'd ever met, and he considered him his father—his *only* father. Flood might not have sired him, but he'd raised him with love and respect, and Luke owed everything to him. Sadness gripped him each time he thought Flood was hurting. That hadn't much crossed his mind before.

"Pa," Luke began, but stopped when his voice cracked. "Pa," he said again, feeling all of six years old, when he'd broken the lamp off his father's desk, the one his mother had given to him at Christmas. Luke reached out and grasped Flood's arm. "Fox Dancing is as much a surprise to me as she is to you and everyone else. Especially Ma. I hope you understand I don't try to cause strife in the family—at least not anymore. Those days are behind me. But here I am again, just like when I was a boy. You and Ma always had your hands full, but you never made me feel different. I made myself do that. I never—"

"Hush, Luke. That's life. Just when you think you have it figured out, or believe that things are smooth sailing from years of work, circumstances take an unexpected turn and knock the wind from your sail." He shook his head and gave a sad chuckle. "I guess things would get pretty boring if they didn't."

Flood turned toward the barn, but Luke caught his arm. "What about you and Ma?"

His father straightened. "What about us?"

"There's just this thing between you—ever since Fox Dancing showed up. I can feel it."

Flood nodded slowly. "Just another incident of life I— *we*—have to deal with. As hard as it is for me to think of Claire during the time she spent in captivity with the Cheyenne, I have to remember she was not at fault—for any of her actions or feelings."

Luke wondered at the way Flood said the last word. Maybe his father knew more than his mother thought he did.

"We'll work it through, son. We always do." He shrugged. "But I appreciate you asking."

Flood was a fighter. He hadn't built this wild land into the successful ranch he now owned by being a pushover.

Changing the subject, Luke said, "I still can't get over how Fox Dancing found her way here by herself. Most whites still believe the only good Indian is a dead Indian."

"I wonder who the young buck was. With the trouble over in Pine Grove, the whole community is sure to be riled when word gets out."

Luke nodded. "She knew him. The look on her face said it all."

"We best keep our eyes open and our noses to the ground. Perhaps we can avert any trouble before it happens."

Luke felt a smile pulling across his face. Here was the man he knew. Always looking on the right side of getting things done. If he could be half the man his pa was, he'd die a happy cowboy. "I'll spread the word around the hands."

Flood clapped him on the back and they started toward the house. Luke hoped it would be that easy, but his gut told him that wasn't the case. Added to this trouble, if he could call it that, was Brandon and Charity. The Heart of the Mountains was once again the eye of the storm.

Chapter Twenty-Nine

By the time they arrived at the Biscuit Barrel, there was hardly a table left to find. Charity glanced around with a fake smile plastered to her face. Her mother had absolutely forbidden her to stay home.

She spotted Luke's table in the far corner, next to Matt's growing family, and Mark's smaller table on the opposite side. Chance and Evie sat with Tobit at a table next to Norman, Ina, Hayden, and a pretty, dark-haired woman who must be his wife. She was chatting with Evie, seemingly delighted to be together again. Charity didn't see Fox Dancing. Luke must have realized she'd cause a stir and left her home. But not even her tough cowboy brothers could withstand the barrage of their children and wives begging to attend the Wednesday night special at the café.

She followed her parents across the room toward the other McCutcheons, happy, and yet melancholy too. She'd never feel whole again until Brandon returned, if he ever did.

Faith waved. "Over here, Flood and Claire." She gave Charity an extraspecial smile. "We saved some places at our tables, but you'll have to split up. It's a full house already, even though it's still early. Make up your mind quickly and order, before they run out of boysenberry."

Faith knew that was Charity's favorite. Several servers scurried around the room, pouring water, coffee, and in some instances, milk. Each wore a blue plaid peasant dress and had her hair fashioned on top of her head. The owners, Mr. and Mrs. Larson, prided themselves on having pretty young woman working for them—a ploy to draw in the men. Charity sometimes wondered if that was one of the reasons her family, dominated by men, had chosen this place for their weekly get-together. She wouldn't doubt it. That, and the sweet aroma in the warm room smelled heavenly.

Luke stood and pulled out the chair next to Faith and seated her. Her ma and pa split up between Matt's and Mark's tables.

"Where's Fox Dancing?" she asked, leaning close to Faith. Colton was to her left, and Dawn sat next to him on Luke's other side. Luke also held Holly.

"Luke thought it best if she stayed home tonight, and she agreed. Lucky promised to stop in to see if she needed anything in an hour or so—so she won't feel so alone or get frightened."

Charity laughed. "I don't think much scares her."

"That's probably true. Still, she's young and in an unfamiliar place. Did she ever say if she knew the Indian brave?"

Charity nodded. "Yes. I asked her in the barn today after it happened. From the little I could understand, he is from her tribe, and may even be a suitor. Or was. I'm not quite sure. From her reaction, I could tell she didn't want to talk with me about him. Maybe she thinks we'll do him harm. I don't know. She was just as surprised as we were when he showed up."

It had been a while since Charity had seen the Biscuit Barrel this busy. The sight of Reverend Crittlestick brought thoughts of the wedding and almost cemented a lump in her throat. But she was learning she was a heck of a lot stronger than she thought she was when Brandon rode out. She gave a wave when the reverend looked over and smiled. Berta May, sitting with him, was set to come out to the ranch tomorrow for a second fitting of her mother's wedding dress. Charity wondered if she should call it off until she knew more.

Several minutes later, the waitress brought dishes laden with large slices of pies of all kinds. She and Faith had gotten the last two slices of boysenberry.

"Hello, Charity."

Brandon!

A dark shadow of whiskers covered his square jaw, and his dark, expressive eyes were hooded. What did that mean? Had he taken the job? Fear mingled in her stomach with excitement and joy. The chatter in the room quieted. Seemed everyone was anxious to hear what he had to say.

She struggled to swallow quickly. "Brandon."

He held out his hand. "Can we speak outside?"

How could she say no? She fought the urge to seek out her mother's face, or Luke's, or anyone else's in her family. She had to stop running to everyone else to make her decisions for her. Nodding, she let him help her up and walked through the quiet room, everyone's gazes still glued to their backs.

Fox Dancing ran to her bedroom window when she heard a stone tap against it, followed by another. She struggled to get the contraption open, but when she couldn't seem to make it work, she placed her warm palm on the clear barrier and looked out into the night. It didn't take long to spot Painted

Bear Stone standing below her window. He must have watched everyone leave in the wagon earlier.

Their gazes locked, and a chill slipped up her spine. Never in her wildest imaginings had she expected him to follow her. But he had. And he was here. When she'd seen him in the struggle with the white boy-man, she'd nearly flung herself on him to get him to stop. If he'd killed the white man, he'd have been hung.

Turning, she ran through her room, down the hall and stairway, and flung open the front door. Once she was outside, she stopped and gathered her runaway emotions and approached Painted Bear Stone slowly, stopping a few feet away. Anger, and something else, burned deep in his wide-set eyes.

"You are *my* wife, and you run off like a child," he said in their native tongue. It wasn't a question, only an angry complaint. "The agreement was made and horses delivered."

He stepped forward, but she held her ground.

"You have disgraced me. I have the right to kill you this moment if I choose it so." He pulled his long knife from its sheath. The blade glimmered in the moonlight.

She held her head high and nodded. "Yes!" she retorted. "And I will disgrace you *again* if you try to take me back. Go find another wife from among the young women of the tribe. Someone who desires to be trapped inside a tepee to cook your food, sew robes to hang over your shoulders, or have your children. Because I do not! I am also a warrior—just like you! I have made my vision quest and killed a bear on my own." She thought of the scar that spanned her back from approaching the animal she thought dead. "That should prove to you that I am serious. You should have taken my word when I told you I had no interest, before asking my father."

Why doesn't he look convinced?

He came a step closer, his eyes glittering, but she was not frightened. This was Painted Bear Stone. He would do anything to keep her safe, as he had since childhood, even follow her through the white man's land where they were not welcome. His mouth pulled down and his eyes took in every detail. She felt her spirit bending toward his, and she jerked her thoughts away.

"We will leave now. Before the rest return."

"Did you see him?" Fox Dancing asked, unable to keep her excitement over Luk quiet another moment. "He's just like Father said, an important white man among his people. He's kind too. Though he was surprised when—"

"I saw not a white man and not a red man," he interrupted curtly. "I saw a man with one foot in both worlds."

His tone cut like flint and she winced. He didn't care about her brother, only about getting her back to the village, where she would become his property. Before she knew what he was about, he reached out and grasped her wrist, pulling her to the hard muscles of his chest.

"Don't put up a fight, Fox Dancing. It is time to return to your world."

At the sound of hoofbeats, Painted Bear Stone looked around.

Not knowing who it was, she placed her hand on his arm; the warm sensation under her fingertips surprised her. Fear for him made her voice hard. "Go! You are not safe!" Using the distraction, she jerked out of his grasp, darted into the house, and slammed the door.

Chapter Thirty

As soon as they walked out the door, Charity vaulted into Brandon's arms. Keenly aware of everyone watching through the windows, Brandon took time to hold her, relishing the feel. For a moment he closed his eyes, thanking God for this beautiful woman who still loved him even though he'd gone off half-cocked on a wild goose chase all the way to Kansas City and back.

"You're back so soon," she said against his neck. "I wasn't expecting you for another week, or more."

"You complaining?" he teased.

"Never."

"Good." He set her away. "Walk with me. Everyone's watching. I think we've given them enough gossip fodder for a year, and then some."

He took her hand in his and started down the street.

"It didn't take but a few minutes in Kansas City for me to know I had to get back to Y Knot—and you—or lose my mind," he said as they strolled down the boardwalk. "When I finally came to my senses, there was still an early train Monday morning, and I wasn't going to let it leave without me."

They stopped in front of Lou and Dritt's boardinghouse. He turned and went up the walk. The inside of the inn was dimly lit, with one light burning in the window. He heard a murmur of voices from inside.

"Let's sit out here on the porch. Lou won't mind."

He sat Charity in one chair and pulled another chair close. "First things first," he said, finding her lips. The strength with which she kissed him back surprised him. He gathered his emotions, then pulled back.

"I couldn't do it, Charity. The moment I arrived, I started wishing you were there. Everything I saw, I wished I was sharing with you. Deep in my heart, I knew it wouldn't be right to take you from the ranch, even if you would go. You belong out here." He glanced down the walk at the quiet street, the only sounds coming from the Hitching Post Saloon a couple doors to their right or the Biscuit Barrel on their left.

He liked it. The quiet. And the multitude of stars he could see overhead. "Kansas City was dirty and crowded. Every place I went, every person I met, I was comparing it to what I have here." He looked deep into her eyes. "Tell me I still have you, Charity. That you still love me. That's been my deepest fear, that I'd come home and you would have changed your mind."

A beautiful smile graced her face, meant only for him. "I love you with all my heart, Brandon. I never stopped, and I never will. I prayed every night you'd come home, but still, I only wanted that if it would make you happy."

Unable to stop himself, he wrapped her in his arms again. "That's music to my ears, darlin'. You've made me a happy man. I know my place and I won't ever doubt again. The feelings I was imagining about Timberlake were only that. Figments of my fancy. Wishes of what I'd lost as a boy and what never could be again. I'm not a kid anymore, and I don't want to be. You're the only thing that is important to me. Wherever you are, I'll be happy."

The door creaked open and he sat back, looking through the darkness.

"Who's out there?" Lou called softly. "I hear voices."

"It's me and Charity, Lou," Brandon replied.

"Sheriff?"

"That's right. We needed a private place to talk. Thought you and Dritt wouldn't mind us using your porch."

"Of course we don't mind. Consider it yours, anytime you'd like."

Brandon chuckled. "That's kind of you, Lou. After the wedding, we may take you up on that offer, being as how my tiny front porch only has an unromantic view of the jailhouse."

He heard her softly closing the front door and crossing the porch. "That's *wonderful* news," she said. "From what I heard the last few days, I was afraid the wedding wasn't going to take place after all."

Brandon felt Charity stiffen. The poor girl. She'd suffered so much humiliation she didn't deserve, all because of him. He hoped he'd be able to make it up to her. "Yes, it's happening. And we can hardly wait—but of course we are."

She cleared her throat. "Yes, of course you are."

Charity pulled on his arm. He let a few moments slip by so Lou would get the hint.

"Well, I'll be going on in. You sit out here as long as you like—anytime."

"Thank you," Charity said softly, a bit of her fervor seeming to have evaporated.

When the door closed softly, he pulled her close. "I'm sorry, honey. I know this hasn't been easy for you. I'll make it up to you, I promise."

"There's nothing to make up. I'm just relieved you went and found out now, before the wedding. Maybe if it happened after our wedding, you would have always wondered what life would be like as a marshal. You never told me about Timberlake himself. What was the man like? Was he what you thought he'd be?"

A moment passed as he gathered his thoughts. What would Charity think when she found out he'd never spoken with the man? Would her feelings change? Only one way to find out. "I never got that far."

"What?"

"When I went to Timberlake's office for the interview, he wasn't there. His deputy told me that he hadn't even mentioned my coming, and that he talked about hiring new deputies all the time. I'd all but made my decision to return the day I arrived, so when I heard that bit of news, I was happy to say my good-byes and head straight for the train depot. I couldn't get home to Y Knot fast enough."

"I'm sorry, Brandon. You never even spoke with him?"

He shook his head. "I don't care about the past, honey. I regret the grief I've caused you."

She glanced down at their hands twined together. "Only two more weeks, and then I'll be living with you in town, cooking your dinners and being with you every day." Her gaze, now trained steadily on his own, spoke of love and commitment that would last a lifetime. "I can hardly wait."

"I know the feeling, darlin'. Two weeks can't go fast enough to suit me."

When Luke pulled the wagon to a halt in front of the house and saw Lucky's horse still tied at the hitching rail, unease snaked up his spine. Before he even had a chance to circle around the back to assist Faith and the young'uns, the door opened and Lucky rushed out to meet him.

"What is it, Lucky? Has something happened?"

"From what I can figure out, that young buck that Francis had a tussle with returned and carted her off."

"What? Fox Dancing is gone?"

Lucky nodded. "I've been waiting for you to get back for an hour. I showed up, just like you asked. The door was ajar and there looks like there was a struggle. Faith, one of your lanterns in the front room got busted," he said, looking up at her. "And some other stuff. That young sister of yours put up quite the fight."

Luke ran into the house, knowing Lucky would help Faith with the children. He took the stairs two at a time. The bedroom was just as it was when they'd left earlier that evening. While he was out having pie and talking up a good time, Fox Dancing had been abducted by that Cheyenne brave. He wished he'd taken the time to find out more about him than the little bit Fox Dancing had shared with Charity. She'd seemed happy here and hadn't shown any interest in following the brave. He was sure she'd been taken against her will. And as far as clues went, he had very little to go on.

He returned to the front room to find Faith and the children, along with Lucky, taking in the scene. The carpet was askew and a chair toppled over. By the window, he squatted down to touch a small round spot.

Blood.

Whatever happened, one of them had been hurt.

"Lucky, I'd like you to stay here with Faith. When I get to the main house I'll send over Uncle Pete, and Pedro too."

Faith watched him intently. "What are you going to do?"

"Not sure yet. Go alert the others for now. Get together a search party. Find Fox Dancing."

Chapter Thirty-One

With both hands wrapped around the cold, steely bars on her windows, Fox Dancing gazed out into the night, a burning pit of fear in her stomach almost making her retch. Her talisman was gone. Angry with herself, she pushed away her weakness. She was a warrior. She would get free, even if she had to kill someone to do it.

When a man she'd never seen before had stepped into Luk's dwelling as if he owned the place, suspicion blossomed. He'd told her to come, and when she refused, he'd tried to grasp her wrist. They'd wrestled, bumping into things, smashing a lamp. The foul-smelling man was large. And strong. She had no weapon. That was the last thing she remembered before waking up in this place. Her skin crawled when she realized he must have held her unconscious body while traveling.

A sharp pain in her head made her wince. She reached up and fingered a lump on the side of her head. What happened now? Would Luk come looking for her?

She left the rock wall with the window and crossed her enclosure. With a light touch, she felt around as high as she could, searching for a way out. She thought of her father and what he would do. Her grandfather's face swam before her gritty eyes, making her heart clench, but she pushed away the emotion. Dim starlight from outside was her only lamp.

A violent shiver took hold of her body and she clenched her jaw tightly, wishing for her buffalo robe back home in her tepee. Where was Painted Bear Stone? Had he witnessed her abduction or had he already left to travel back to the village without her?

She felt naked without the amulet. She hadn't removed it since her vision quest. Discouraged, cold, and nursing a growing anger, she sank down onto a ragged cot along the wall. Leaning forward, she cradled her head in her hands. She'd never seen a hanging, but she knew the whites were all too eager to rid themselves of Indians. Would her journey to find her brother prove to be her death?

The sound of several men's voices carried, followed by coarse laughter. Her breathing quickened, knowing that it wouldn't be long before something very evil happened—she was sure of it. Would she be strong, or cry and beg for her life?

At the familiar sharp cry of a hawk, she started. She rushed to the window, a jolt of happiness propelling her feet. Blackness covered everything. Across the street, next to the wall of a building, she could make out Painted Bear Stone's silhouette.

Just outside the front door of the main house, Brandon dipped his head for one last kiss. He traced his lips across Charity's. After their discussion on Lou and Dritt's front porch, he and Charity had gone back to the Biscuit Barrel, hand in hand. After a slice of pie of his own, he'd ridden home in the buggy with Charity and her parents, his horse tied behind.

Luke thundered into the yard. "Brandon," he yelled before dismounting. "I'm glad you're still here."

He turned, Charity at his side. "What's going on?"

"Something's happened while we were in town. Looks like someone rode onto McCutcheon land and carted off Fox Dancing from my house. Furniture was upset and it looked like there'd been a struggle. She was gone when Lucky stopped over to check on her."

"Could it be the Indian brave who fought with Francis?" Charity asked, concern making her voice crack.

"That's exactly who I think it is," Luke answered. "If there hadn't been a struggle, I would have assumed she'd gone willingly, lonesome for her home. But not now."

Charity had told him how the brave showed up and fought with Francis. They wouldn't find two lone Indians if that male didn't want to be found. It would be like searching for a yellow petal in a field of daisies. Luke wasn't going to like what he had to say.

"You realize it's highly unlikely we'll be able to find them. Especially with the lead time they've had. He'll take her and disappear into the land, where we won't be able to follow."

Luke shot him a hard look. "I'm not giving up as easy at that. I'm going to at least try."

"I didn't say I wasn't going to try. Just didn't want you to get your hopes up."

"And if it were Charity?"

"Yeah, I know."

The front door opened and Claire came out, followed by Flood. "What's going on?" Claire asked. Flood stood back.

"Fox Dancing is missing," Charity said, her lips still puffy from his kisses. "Let me help search as well, Brandon. I can track as good as any man."

"Not on your life," he responded. "You stay here with your mother." Flood had already gone back inside to get his hat and gun. "We'll gather the hands in the bunkhouse and fan out on Luke's land, looking for tracks. Until light, we may not spot much. If he wants to get lost, he'll head for the hills, and so will we."

"But Brandon—"

Her mother grasped Charity's hand. "Listen to him, Charity. I don't want to be worrying over you. He'll move faster, and with a clearer head, if you're safe here at home with me."

It didn't take long before the whole bunkhouse was roused and cowboys poured out, heading for the horse corral. In mere minutes, the animals were saddled and the group mounted up.

After breaking the men into three groups and giving them his instructions, Brandon strode over to Charity, waiting a few feet away. He turned her away so the others couldn't see, and kissed her passionately. "I'm gettin' tired of waiting. When this gets resolved, we're gettin' hitched—and I don't care who likes it or not!"

The twinkle in her blue eyes was enough to fuel his fire. She ran her hands up his chest. "I agree wholeheartedly, Sheriff. I'll be waiting. But for now, just find Fox Dancing and bring her back."

Chapter Thirty-Two

Charity tossed and turned, her bed feeling like a quarry of rocks instead of a soft mattress. It had been several hours since the men had ridden out, and a deep foreboding, something she couldn't describe, kept her awake and staring through the darkness at the beams above her head. Sitting up, she reached over and lit her lantern. The clock said one. Was her mother awake too? Maybe she should go down and make a cup of tea, check to see that she was all right.

Charity pulled on her wrapper and picked up her bedside lantern. The hall was dark. As she rounded the upstairs landing, the soft glow of the lantern they'd left burning in the downstairs window chased away the darkness of the night. She was halfway down the stairs when a bloodcurdling scream reverberated from the kitchen, almost causing Charity to stumble.

Esperanza!

Grasping the lamp tightly, Charity hurried down the staircase as fast as she could without falling. Was her mother in the kitchen as well? What was happening? A terrifying quiet descended over the house.

Without a thought for her safety, Charity ran through the kitchen door, then skidded to a stop. Her mother stood in the middle of the room with a large kitchen knife pointed at the tall, well-muscled Indian who had fought with Francis yesterday. Esperanza was huddled behind her.

He stood unafraid. His chin jutted out and his eyes reminded her of coals from a hot fire. As strange as it was, she was certain her mother's knife was not holding him off. In one swoop, he'd be able to disarm her and turn the knife on all of them if he wanted. His bare chest was marked with several large scars.

"Mother, are you all right?" she whispered, not wanting to set him off. "Esperanza?"

The knife in her mother's hands glinted in the light from her lantern. She nodded. "Yes. We're unharmed. We were just heating some water when we turned to find him standing right where he is. I have no idea how he got in."

Charity inched forward, needing to be by her mother's side. Wanting to protect her in case the warrior decided to strike. "Have you seen Fox Dancing? Is she here with him somewhere?"

Claire shook her head. Esperanza's face was deadly white and Charity feared the housekeeper might fall and strike her head on the counter behind her.

"Can I go?" Charity spoke to the Indian while nodding toward the women.

He didn't respond, but neither did he try to stop her when she slowly walked forward and set her lantern on the counter. How she wished she had the gun she'd left upstairs in her room. Who thought you'd need a weapon in your own home?

Charity took Esperanza's shoulders just as she swayed, and guided her to a stool close by, while her mother kept the knife pointed on the intruder. She patted Esperanza's cheeks, not wanting her to pass out.

"You're fine, Esperanza. Take a few deep breaths. Everything is going to be all right."

I hope that's true.

"I think you should put the knife down, Mother," she said. "If he were going to hurt us, he would have already."

When Charity reached out and took the weapon, laying it next to the lamp, the Indian stepped forward. Her mother gasped, the first sign she was frightened. Was she remembering the day she'd been abducted? Charity put her arms around her and held her tight.

"Look at him, Mother. I think he wants to tell us something. I don't think he wants to hurt us."

In a low, slow tone, the Indian said a few soft words. Charity wished she could understand. Then he held something out to her. In the dim light, she would have to cross the room a few steps to see what it was. Her mother tried to hold her back, but Charity calmed her fears with a soft look.

"I think he's our friend. Let me see what he's trying to tell us."

Close enough now, she immediately understood. "It's Fox Dancing's amulet." The Indian pointed to the back door. "He wants me to go with him. Maybe she's hurt and needs help."

"Charity, if you do, we may lose you forever. You could be held captive or killed. I won't let you."

Charity turned. "I have to go. For Luke. And for Fox Dancing. He's not going to hurt me."

The Cheyenne brave pointed to her mother, then back at her. "Mother, he wants us both."

Claire nodded, the need to protect her daughter seeming to have calmed her fears. "You're right. That young girl needs us. Let me gather my things."

Mounted on her palomino mare, and her mother on her bay gelding, they rode silently behind the large, muscular Appaloosa that resembled Fox Dancing's horse. Charity hadn't said anything to her mother, but concern had begun building when they'd left Y Knot's surrounding area. Soon, if they stayed in this direction, they would reach Pine Grove. Had Fox Dancing's horse fallen again, leaving her seriously hurt near the town? If yes, this young man leading them wouldn't be able to approach just anyone safely. And because of it, he'd ridden all the way back to their ranch.

When he pulled to a stop, they rode alongside. He put his finger to his lips and leaned in. They were along the outlying streets, hidden back in the foliage. He murmured something, then looked at Claire.

"He's trying to tell us something," Charity said to her mother, who still looked nervous.

The Indian said a few more words. Her mother listened, then cut her gaze to Charity. "I'm not sure. I think he's trying to say 'jail.'"

Charity quickly pointed to her gun, then traced a star on her chest, where Brandon always pinned his.

The Indian nodded.

"Yes. Sheriff Huxley must have Fox Dancing locked up in a cell."

She dismounted and handed her reins up to her mother. She crept through the bushes until she could see the street. The sturdy brick jailhouse was alive with light. Two men came out and went up the street in the opposite direction. She hurried back to where the others waited.

"The jail is lit up like the Fourth of July," she whispered. "They must have Fox Dancing inside."

After an uncomfortable glance at the Indian, her mother dismounted too. "Why would they take her? I don't understand."

"I don't know either, but I'm going to find out. I'll go down and scout it out. Can you tell him?" She pointed to the brave still astride his horse.

"That'll be very dangerous, Charity. Men worked up over Indian trouble are not usually thinking straight."

"I know. That's why we have to hurry, in case they have bad intent. I didn't see Sheriff Huxley. I wonder if he's even there. He came out to the ranch the other day wanting to talk with her."

Claire looked around. "I should go with you."

"No, you need to stay here. Just in case things don't go well. You might have to ride for help. I'm not going to do anything foolish, just see if she's there. You stay for backup. He'll not hurt you."

When they both glanced at the brave, he gave a wan smile, as if he knew what she'd just said.

"Mother, if I'm not back in twenty minutes, go to Stef Hannessy, owner of the Night Owl Mine, and have one of his men ride for the others. If Brandon were here, we wouldn't have a thing to worry about."

"I'm not so sure about that," her mother responded. "Men are strange creatures. When it comes to Indians, or Indian lovers, it doesn't take much…"

Charity gasped. "You don't think it will come to that, do you? These are our neighbors and friends. They wouldn't dare do anything to me."

"At this point in my life, I don't put anything past anyone. I wish Flood were here."

They embraced.

"You be careful, my brave daughter. Come back to me safe and sound."

Chapter Thirty-Three

With a walnut-sized lump in her throat, Charity slunk along the boardwalk, staying in the shadows and close to the walls, the weight of her six-gun, strapped to her thigh, giving her courage. Thank goodness for guns. How she wished she'd had one that night a few weeks ago in Rio Wells, when she'd been faced with the malevolent bank owner who'd wanted her dead.

Actually, she wished she had more than her gun that night, like a skirt or a pair of pants. Running out into a sleeping Rio Wells in only her bloomers when she'd spotted Brandon riding down the road had been a pretty harebrained thing to do.

At the memory, she almost smiled, but pushed it away when two men came out of the jailhouse, turned on their heel, then hurried off down the street in the opposite direction.

In front of the bakeshop a good block away from the jailhouse, she stopped. Watched and listened. The place, still lit up, seemed deserted. Five minutes passed without anyone around. Where had they all gone? Was Fox Dancing really locked away inside—or was this a mistake? Her brothers wouldn't hesitate in the slightest. They'd meet whoever, and whatever, straight on. She'd learned to use her firearm right along with them. She wasn't frightened, at least not much.

Having talked herself into the positive outcome, she walked down the dark street confidently and crossed the threshold. The room was empty. Nervously, she fingered the gun on her hip, then, when no one showed up, she opened the door to the back room and the cells.

Fox Dancing bolted to her feet. She rushed the bars, rattling off several long sentences, none of which Charity could understand. The girl blinked several times, and Charity saw a glimmer of tears in her eyes.

"Luk?"

Charity shook her head. "No. Sorry. Just me and Ma and…" She thought a moment. With her hands, she made the outline of the Indian's body and then pointed to her. "A really big man."

Fox Dancing's gaze cut away and she stared disappointedly at the floor. They both knew they needed Luke, and the other McCutcheons, before things got out of hand.

With no one around, this might be her only opportunity to do something to save Fox Dancing. She reached in her pocket, took out the talisman the Indian brave had given her, and passed it to Fox Dancing through the bars. The girl slipped it over her head.

"Wait here." Charity shook her head when she realized how that sounded. "I'll be right back." She hurried into the main room and went over to Huxley's desk. She scanned the top, looking for the keys. She needed to hurry. It wouldn't do to get caught trying to break Fox Dancing out.

Unsuccessful, she opened the top drawer, finding it so stuffed with junk, she was sure the keys couldn't be there. Same with the next two.

There weren't any other places in the room that could hold the key ring. A coatrack by the door was loaded with several coats and a slicker. She crossed the room and patted down each garment. When she felt a hard ridge, she pulled the coat aside to find the keys hanging on a hook behind the clothes. A good hiding place—one that had almost fooled her.

Excited, Charity had a difficult time getting the key in the lock. Once in, the clumsy old mechanism didn't want to turn. Sweat, born of desperation, broke out on her forehead. She gripped the key with both hands and strained, twisting it with all she had. The satisfying clink of the lock giving way met their ears.

She looked up at Fox Dancing and smiled—only to see the girl's eyes riveted on the door.

"Going somewhere?"

Charity whirled.

A man had a gun trained at her chest. She slowly raised her hands, silently cursing her impulsiveness. She should have gathered the information like she'd planned, and got her tail back to her mother.

The pot-bellied man with the greasy black mustache stepped forward and slipped her gun from her holster. He smelled foul. His small, beady eyes didn't miss a thing.

"Where's Sheriff Huxley?" she demanded. "I want to speak with him right away!"

The man sneered, then looked her up and down in the most disgusting way.

"Ain't here."

"Well, go find him!"

"Shut up and get in that cell." He pointed with his gun. "Unless you want me to shoot you right here and now."

"I'm Charity McCutcheon. You have no right to put me in jail!"

"I got every right, girlie McCutcheon. You was breakin' my prisoner out. Had the door open. If I hadn't shown up when I did, you two would be long gone." His eyes narrowed. "Now *get* your backside inside unless you want that to be your last breath."

It was true. She'd been caught red-handed. She'd not buffalo her way out of this one.

She stepped inside, next to Fox Dancing, and he slammed the door so hard it hurt her ears. The click, when he turned the lock, felt as if she'd been pushed into a bottomless pit.

What about her mother, alone in the woods with the Indian brave? She'd be frightened when Charity didn't come back. Would she be able to find Stef Hannessy's place?

She needed to try something else. "Sir?" she said as politely as she could. He'd just put the key in his pocket and turned to leave. It galled her to have to humble herself for this piece of dung, but desperate times called for desperate measures.

He turned back. "You have a question?" he said in a sweet tone, mocking her own.

"Well, yes. I believe I do. But first, I want to say that I made a horrible mistake in coming in here like I did. I'm sorry. I didn't mean any harm."

When he chuckled, she felt her face go hot. *Why, the big, bumbling backside of a...* "I was just wondering why you had Fox Dancing locked up in your cell in the first place. The last time I saw her, she was at my brother's ranch—you know, my brother, *Luke McCutcheon* from Y Knot?"

An ugly light flared up in the man's eyes. "Guess *your brother* didn't know that he was harboring a murdering Indian fugitive. He wouldn't do a thing like that on purpose, I wouldn't reckon." He took two steps toward the door.

She reached out through the bars, feeling helpless. "Wait!"

When he turned back stern-faced, she added softly, in the most delicate voice she could muster, "Please don't go."

"I got things to do."

"Why do you think she killed someone?"

"A bow and quiver was found at the cabin of two men who were murdered in cold blood. She's the only Injun we've got in the area for a while."

"But Sheriff Huxley told the man I'm going to *marry*, Brandon Crawford, the *sheriff of Y Knot*, that those men killed themselves in a shoot-out."

She gripped the bars, wanting to shake them.

"How has the story changed so much?" she demanded hotly, forgetting to be sweet. "Just because she's an Indian and you want to pin it on someone?"

Clearly aggravated with her forwardness, and most likely put off that she wasn't cowered in the corner crying, he came up to the bars and leered. "I'm through jawing with the likes of *you*!"

He was out the door and getting ready to close it, when she yelled, "When will Sheriff Huxley return? I want to speak with him right now! I have rights!"

"We'll go wake him up just as soon as we're finished hanging the murderer, and not a second sooner." He laughed evilly. "Poor ol' man needs his rest. Any more questions for me?" Before she could respond, he slammed the door shut.

She could feel Fox Dancing's gaze riveted to her side. Turning, she shrugged.

"Luk?"

Charity shook her head. "No Luke. Not yet. But we won't give up hope."

Men's voices drew her over to the window. The men she'd seen leaving were riding down the street with several more. One took the rope from his saddle and tossed it over a beam at the saloon. When Fox Dancing started over, Charity took her by the shoulders and turned her around, sitting them together on the small, not-too-nice-smelling cot. Making plans, when you couldn't communicate, would prove difficult. But what plans could they make? Without a gun, or Brandon knowing where they were, the outcome didn't bode well.

Somehow, she had to stop these crazy men. And where was Sheriff Huxley anyway?

Chapter Thirty-Four

Claire McCutcheon sat on a rock and watched the quiet Cheyenne brave, the reins of her horse and Charity's clutched in her palm. He was a large fellow, although he looked young, surely not yet twenty. Along with a huge knife in a dark leather case tied around his waist, he had a bow and a quiver filled with arrows that she was sure he'd use if Fox Dancing were in mortal danger. But against so many guns, he wouldn't stand a chance. Perhaps he knew that and it was the reason he hadn't tried to break Fox Dancing out of the jail.

He'd been perfectly quiet as he squatted next to a tree, watching the jailhouse. He hadn't even once looked her way. It was apparent he was waiting for Fox Dancing's white brother to come spring her without incident. Claire prayed that would be possible.

She glanced up at the early morning stars and was transported back in time—to the Cheyenne village where she'd learned so much about herself. Feelings surged through her. Anxiety over her little boys at home, who needed their mother. Worry for Flood, who would be ripped up with fear for her. The guilt she carried around every day, knowing how she felt about Luke's father after so many months of not being rescued. How it would kill Flood if he knew.

The hoot of an owl brought her back to the hillside overlooking the jailhouse in Pine Grove. At least thirty minutes had passed since Charity had left. She must be in trouble. It would be up to Claire now to get word out, to alert her family to what was happening before it was too late. Resolved to her course of action, she tied the two sets of reins she held to a bush and quietly approached the brave.

He looked around. The darkness kept her from seeing his eyes.

"I must go find help," she said, searching slowly for the correct Cheyenne words.

He tipped his head.

She walked her fingers across her hands. "I must go. Get help." Should she go alone or take him along? Would he go if she asked? "Charity…"

He grunted and looked away. She was on her own—and as capable as anyone else of finding Stef Hannessy's home. She had a gun and she was a McCutcheon. She'd best remember that if she felt her resolve waver.

Back in the Indian village, she'd learned just how hard, how ruthless, she could be if needed. She'd battled for survival the beginning weeks of her abduction. First the gauntlet, the whippings from the other women, being starved for days and staked out at night like an animal. She'd done better than survive. She'd fought back, learned the language, proven herself worthy of one of the leading braves. Pride for how well she'd done blossomed in her heart. Was that wrong? She didn't know. She'd surprised herself back then, and sometimes she hadn't been able to stop a smile from curling her lips in the moments right before sleep, knowing that Flood would also be proud of her. By the end of her stay, she was a respected part of the community—one worth many, many horses in trade. Now it was time to test her mettle here. She'd not let her family or the Cheyenne down.

Her thoughts drifted to Flood and all they'd been through over the years. All the love they'd shared. How she loved him. If something happened in the next few hours, this could be her last night on earth. She didn't think so, but it was a sobering thought. In a few moments she'd be all alone, riding through the dark Montana night. The contemplation of death made one realize just how wonderful life was, even with its many ups and downs. She wished she'd told him today that she loved him. All that he meant to her. Thinking about her life, she knew she wouldn't change a thing.

The Cheyenne brave stood when she turned, and he walked with her when she went to her horse's side and gathered her reins.

Cupping his hands together, he waited for her to put her boot in so he could give her a leg up. "Go," he said in English.

"Plan on being back in the saddle in ten minutes," Brandon shouted, reining up in the McCutcheon yard with the rest of the men, intent on saddling fresh mounts. He pushed his hand through his hair in frustration, then repositioned his Stetson and pulled it snug on his head. Searching before they had any light was really a waste of time, but there was no stopping Luke. Perhaps they'd get lucky. Spot something that would point them in the right direction.

The ranch door banged open and Brandon turned, expecting Charity. With this many men about, she was sure to hear the racket and wake up. Luke, Matt, Roady, and Smokey all whipped around at Esperanza's shaky call.

"What is it?" Luke asked, walking toward her. Brandon and the rest followed him over.

The housekeeper appeared overwrought with anxiety, moaning and wringing her hands.

"Has something happened? Where's Ma? And Charity?"

The woman was shaking so hard she could barely talk. "She, they—the Indian…"

"Take a deep breath," Matt instructed, putting a calming hand on the woman's arm. "Just tell us what occurred."

A deep, burning fear gripped Brandon's gut. It was almost as if he knew what she was about to say before she spoke.

The housekeeper bit her bottom lip. "Mrs. McCutcheon get up after midnight and come to kitchen for tea. I help. We hear a noise and see Indian in room. I scream. Charity come down. She say he's trying to help Indian girl." Her eyes grew as round as saucers. "They go with him."

The men exchanged a look, then Luke bit out a heated curse, matched by one from Matt. Roady's face all but turned white. Brandon felt as if he'd been hit over the head with a two-by-four. Fear for Charity and Claire burned like searing chunks of coal in his chest.

"They went *willingly*?"

Esperanza nodded.

"Did they say where they were headed?" Luke gritted through clenched teeth. "It took my pa a year to find my ma the first time this happened. We're not losing them a second time!"

Tears sprang into the housekeeper's eyes and she shook her head.

Glancing over his shoulder, Brandon saw Smokey had gone to the corral and was almost finished saddling fresh horses.

"Have any of the others been back here yet?" Matt asked.

Again Esperanza shook her head.

With nothing to go on, they'd never find Charity and Claire, let alone Fox Dancing. Brandon needed to get to his horse, do something.

He hurried over and finished tacking the animal. They mounted. "I'm going into Y Knot to see if Jack knows anything. Luke, you come with me. Matt, you and Roady head to Grassy Gulch and see if anyone has spotted them. Smokey, you ride toward Waterloo. Esperanza, if Flood and the others show up, tell them what you told us and the places we're headed. You got that?"

She nodded.

"I'm sure they'll fan out in the opposite directions, covering the widest territory possible. We all best pray we can find them before they get too far."

Charity hadn't stopped asking for Sheriff Huxley since she'd been locked up. About two hours had passed, and her voice was hoarse from shouting to the other room, demanding to talk with him. The deputy who had thrown her into the cell had come and gone several times, but mostly she'd been ignored. Sinking down to the cot, she felt the chill of the dank cell settle in her bones. Fox Dancing sat still as stone, staring at the bars as if she could make them vanish. By now, her mother would be back anytime with help.

At the sound of more horses approaching, Charity jumped up and ran to the window.

Her mother! And Stef Hannessy! Arriving just as the sun was coming up. "They made it," she gushed to Fox Dancing. "We'll be released now!"

The Indian girl had stood and followed her to the window. A sound came from her throat when she saw Mrs. McCutcheon. "Luk?" she asked.

"Sorry, Fox Dancing. Still no Luke. But if I know my brother and Brandon, they'll be here soon. You can count on it."

A few muffled words, a deep, accented curse—surely from the tall Swede, Hannessy—and the door separating the chambers from the office opened. Her mother ran over to the cell.

"What's going on, Mother? Are they going to release us?"

At six foot four, Hannessy towered over her mother. Both his and her mother's holsters were conspicuously empty.

"Archie Bly has mush for brains," Hannessy said angrily. "He won't release the girl, says she killed some men. And won't release you, saying you were trying to break her out. He's waiting for Judge Wesley to come through to hear your case."

Charity groaned. "My case? Only me? Did you see the rope they strung up at the saloon?"

"No," her mother replied. "I guess we missed that. When did that happen?"

Charity snagged her gaze. "A couple hours ago."

Deputy Bly ambled in, followed by another man holding a gun. "Time's up. Can't leave you in here all day."

Hannessy turned on the man, his face contorting in anger. "I don't know what you're trying to pull, Deputy, but I'm going to have your badge. What are you planning with the rope at the saloon?"

"I think you can guess. Hanging this redskin for the murder of Drake Greenly and the other man, Smith."

"She hasn't had a trial," Claire said. "That's against the law."

"We found all the evidence we need. Why waste everyone's time just goin' through the motions, when we already know the outcome?"

More excited voices sounded from the front room. Was that Brandon? Or Luke?

"Mother," Charity said quickly. "Did you get a note sent to Y Knot and the ranch, or Brandon—or someone?"

"Not yet. I thought Stef's presence would be enough to get you out." Her mother looked stricken. "I'll go do that now."

If help—*real help*—didn't show up soon...

Charity's insides clenched and she felt her face blanch at what she was thinking, so she shoved the horrific thought away. Fox Dancing needed a miracle, and she needed it fast.

Chapter Thirty-Five

Jack Jones knew nothing about Fox Dancing or Charity and Mrs. McCutcheon, but when he began to tell Brandon about Huxley wanting to question Fox Dancing while he was away in Kansas City, Luke jumped in.

"That's right. Jack rode out to the ranch with him. With you showing up out of the blue tonight, and with everything else happening, that slipped my mind. Maybe Huxley had other intentions than he let on."

Something in Brandon's gut told him Huxley would give them some answers. What those answers were, he didn't know. But anything was better than nothing. Wheeling their horses around, he and Luke thundered for Pine Grove.

"What in the blazes is going on?" Luke shouted to him as they galloped into Pine Grove on sweat-lathered horses. The place was alive with activity. "It looks like a lynching."

Along the street, more than a handful of men, most bleary-eyed and rumpled, stood with torches, watching. Deputy Bly came out of the jailhouse shoving Fox Dancing in front of him, her hands tied behind her back. Her eyes were large and frightened. A ferocious anger ripped through Brandon as he cut his gaze to see Luke's reaction. He'd have his hands full keeping Luke from killing anyone.

Just as he thought, Luke's face was contorted with rage. Brandon drew his gun and fired a shot into the air, making his horse jump sideways. Everyone jerked around to see who had arrived.

"What is this, Bly?" he shouted. He rode straight up to the man, bumping him with his horse, his gun inches from Bly's nose.

Bly stumbled back for a second, but kept Fox Dancing in front of him. His cronies stepped forward to make sure Brandon saw the guns they had trained on him and Luke.

There was more gun pointing going on than at a turkey shoot. This could get plenty ugly, plenty fast. Brandon didn't want Fox Dancing, or any other innocent person, to be killed. He chanced a quick glance around. Claire McCutcheon stood with the local mine owner and another man with a gun keeping them still. Where was Charity?

"Untie her hands," Brandon demanded. "She's done nothing wrong."

"How do you know? I found her bow and arrows up at Drake's claim."

"I searched that place myself and didn't find a thing. Now they mysteriously show up a week later? Who discovered them? You? That's mighty convenient, don't you think? Besides all that, those two men were killed with guns."

Luke rode forward. "I should kill you right now for kidnapping her out of my house, you piece of dung." A murmur went through the men. "What's the matter?" Luke added, glaring pointedly at the saloon rats who were more than happy to participate in a hanging. "Didn't Bly tell you that? He broke the law, and you're all accomplices."

"Where's Huxley?" Brandon yelled, looking around. He didn't like the trapped expression on Bly's face. The Pine Grove deputy still had Fox Dancing in his grasp.

"Over here," a feeble voice called out.

Everyone turned.

Huxley stumbled down the dark street in a nightshirt. He held a bloody rag to his forehead.

"Bly knocked me out cold when I asked what the devil was going on out here."

Huxley's appearance was the distraction Bly needed to pull his gun and put it to Fox Dancing's head.

"Let her go, Archie," Brandon said calmly, calling him by his first name. "You don't want to do this."

The deputy looked crazed. Brandon needed to cool everyone down. He nudged his horse forward, but the scoundrel yanked Fox Dancing's arms higher behind her back, making the frightened girl wince.

"No!" Bly shouted, his face contorting into an ugly sneer. "She's a murdering Indian! Have you forgotten about Drake and Smith? They deserve justice! I should just shoot her now. One way is as good as another."

Fox Dancing tried to keep a firm hold on her fear. She was a warrior! She dug deep for her calm, all the while wishing she had her knife so she could slit this white dog's throat. Her grandfather's voice repeated in her head, instructing her to call on her spirit helper, but with all the shouting and confusion, it was difficult.

She was strong, she could—

The deputy holding her jerked her arms back with force, but she stifled her cry of pain. She felt Luk's eyes on her, firm and confident. She didn't want him to be killed because of her. That would be an injustice she'd not be able to carry—even into the next world. She felt something else too as the masses of men crowded around them, the killing lust in their eyes. Their hate. Their fear.

Painted Bear Stone. He was here somewhere. Someplace close. Her soul rushed with love and regret. She'd held back from him because she believed becoming his wife would change her into a different sort of woman. One who wouldn't be able to ride and hunt. That seemed unthinkable. But now, he was here, and with all the white men about was sure to be killed—*because of her*. Thinking of his face, so stern and strong, brought a surge of emotion. He'd come after her because he *loved* her.

A loud cry echoed through the dark night.

Men jerked around in fear.

Painted Bear Stone, bare chested, his face covered in war paint, leaped from the roof of the building behind her, taking down Bly and knocking her into the dirt.

Joy burst through her—then fear for his life—as she scrambled to her feet. Before anyone could respond, Painted Bear Stone flipped the stunned deputy over and straddled him on the ground. With a firm grip on the ugly man's hair, Painted Bear Stone pressed his knife to the dog's throat.

"Hold your fire!" the man with Luk yelled. His eyes blazed with anger as he shifted his gun from one man to the next. "The first person to fire a shot, I'll take down myself!"

"And I've got his back," Luk hollered. "We won't tell you twice!"

Luk's mother, followed by the tall man who'd come into the jail, ran forward now that their guard had been frightened off.

"Everyone just stay calm. That goes for you too, Luke," the man with Luk yelled.

The look on Luk's face was the most frightening of all.

Painted Bear Stone called out to her, beckoning her close. When the deputy struggled, he pulled the knife slowly across the man's throat, the bright red line of blood standing out on his chalk-white skin.

"Help! He's killin' me!" Bly screamed. "What are ya waitin' for, you fools? Somebody kill this heathen!"

Fox Dancing did her best to block out all the commotion as she listened intently to Painted Bear Stone. At the same time, the tall man with Luk's mother untied her hands. Released, she rubbed her wrists. As best she could, Fox Dancing conveyed what Painted Bear Stone had said to Luk's mother. Painted Bear Stone fished in Bly's pocket. What he pulled out, he placed in Fox Dancing's palm.

Still on his horse, Luk's companion motioned to her that he wanted the object. Taking it, he turned it over in his hands.

Luk's mother addressed the crowd in a loud voice. "This young brave says he saw what happened to the men named Drake and Smith. The man he's holding down came out to their claim on the river. The three men passed around a bottle of whiskey until it was gone. After that, they argued. He heard the words *money* and *poker*. The man called Drake stomped away toward the forest. When he turned back to say something, Bly picked up a gun and shot him. Bly shot the other man next, even though he pleaded for his life. Bly stole the money from their pockets and a sack of gold dust from their dwelling. He went away satisfied. The brave followed him. Bly found the quiver and bow lost by Fox Dancing. When he came upon the calf, he killed it for sport, nothing else."

Luk's mother took a deep breath and cast an angry glare at the man Painted Bear Stone held down.

"After Bly left, Painted Bear Stone extracted the arrows, intending to return them to Fox Dancing. Then, suspicious of Bly's intentions, and knowing white men would be quick in blaming an Indian, he removed all tracks, hoping the kill would not be discovered before the wolves and coyotes carried it away."

Finished with the explanation, Luk's mother glanced at Fox Dancing, who nodded.

"This money clip, inscribed with DG, is ironclad evidence, Bly." Luk's friend turned it over once more. "It matches the belt Drake Greenly was wearing when I examined him at the undertaker's. The story couldn't be clearer."

"Bly *has* been throwing a lot of money around," someone shouted from the crowd.

"It ain't true!" Bly screamed. "It's all made up!" He struggled, but Painted Bear Stone held him down easily.

Luk dismounted and walked forward. Bly's cries died in his throat. "You think you can pass your sins off on my little sister—"

"Wait, Luke!" the silver-starred man ordered, his agitated horse still dancing around. He seemed to be the only one Luk would listen to. "What I don't understand is why, all of a sudden, Bly decided the story about them killing each other wasn't enough. Something must have spooked him. Pushed him to cast suspicion elsewhere. We never even thought the calf and the men were connected. But he saw the opportunity to get everyone riled up over an Indian and pass her off as

Drake and Smith's murderer. She'd be hung—taking all suspicion away from him."

The old man with the bloody rag to his head staggered forward. "I know what agitated the two-faced skunk. I began wondering about the second gun. To have a shootout, with the distance the bodies were found from each other, there'd more than likely have to be two weapons—and I only recovered one."

Luk's friend groaned. "Huxley, you never said there was only one gun! Don't you think that was a pretty important piece of the puzzle to leave off?"

"What'd you say, Crawford? I didn't catch that."

"Hey, out there! Hello! What's going on? Somebody come let me out!"

Luk's companion swiveled around. "Charity?"

An hour later, with Painted Bear Stone already mounted and waiting, Fox Dancing slipped into her brother's protective arms. Exhilarated at having found him at last, but also very sad about leaving him behind, she breathed in his unique scent, needing to remember everything. No one knew which way the wind would blow for her people—or how things would turn out. This might be the last time in this world she and her brother would be heart to heart.

She'd already said good-bye to the others, and they waited a few feet away. Painted Bear Stone had tried to give the man with the star his knife, in payment for the two chickens he'd stolen from ranchers while trying to keep out of sight—all while staying as close as he could to Fox Dancing. The man with the star had smiled and refused.

"I'll never forget you," Luk said, still holding her close. "Or that you came all this way to find me. It means more to me than you could ever know."

All she could do was nod, for if she spoke, she'd disgrace herself in a gush of tears.

"This isn't good-bye forever," Luk went on, leaning back so he could look into her face. His mouth pulled down when he saw her tears. "I'll come find you. Someday. And I'll meet our father as well."

Painted Bear Stone grunted out his impatience.

Luk cast him a look. "Take good care of her."

She launched back into Luk's arms and squeezed with all her might. With her cheek against his chest, she choked out a Cheyenne prayer for his safety and that of his family. When her tears began to fall, she jerked away. In three strides, she was at the side of her mare. Taking a handful of her mane, she swung aboard with ease, turned, and galloped off, Painted Bear Stone following behind her.

Chapter Thirty-Six

A soft knock on the bedroom door brought Claire around from the dressing table, where she sat removing her jade earrings.

The door opened slowly.

"Do you have a minute?" Flood asked, standing in the doorway.

"Of course. And since when do you knock?"

Her insides fluttered nervously. Ever since the Pine Grove incident a week ago, when she'd ridden off into the dark night with Charity and the handsome Cheyenne brave named Painted Bear Stone, her nerves had been all the more raw. She wasn't sure why, but it made her sad. Too many memories, she figured. Too numerous and too painful.

"It was a nice ceremony," Flood said, sitting down on the bed. The corners of his lips pulled up. "The sight of that wedding dress brought back all kinds of memories." His gaze found hers, his expression one she couldn't read. Sadness? Uncertainty?

"Did for me too. Candlelight, a big fire in the hearth, snow falling for weeks—and our wedding."

He nodded. "Never thought we'd see the day Brandon and Charity actually wed. Seems like a dream." His chuckle sent a warm pulse of longing through her.

"Well, Jefferson Flood McCutcheon, I can assure you, your daughter is now Mrs. Brandon Crawford. As we speak, she's snuggled in the back of the buggy with her legal husband, on their way to Cattlemen's. I hope we don't see either of their dear faces for a whole week. Think that's asking too much?"

His eyes snagged hers again. Lingered. Made her feel sixteen and falling in love with him all over again.

"Make that two weeks," he said. "After which, we can get back to ranching as usual."

She fiddled nervously with the earring in her fingers. "When will you tell them about the land and the new home to be built?"

"Haven't decided that yet," he replied, rubbing his chin thoughtfully. "When do you think?"

She released the bun on the back of her head and began unbraiding her hair. "After a month or two in the little house. It'll make Charity more appreciative." She couldn't stop her smile, thinking about the surprise. "It's wonderful that everything worked out well with Fox Dancing and Painted Bear Stone. When she finally understood all she had to lose, she realized she couldn't live without him. It was quite romantic."

Flood nodded. "Luke said she even looked excited to be going back. He'll miss her, though."

"I'll miss her as well."

She thought of the emotional parting, and how much Fox Dancing, with the proud tilt to her head and her flashing eyes, resembled her wonderfully complicated third son. But they were dancing around the subject Flood had come in to discuss, she was sure. She could always tell when he had more on his mind by the way he rolled and unrolled his shirtsleeves without realizing he was doing it. His tough exterior wasn't enough to hide his loving heart.

Finished unbraiding and brushing her hair, Claire went over to the bed and sat next to him. The house was quiet. Everyone had departed well fed and happy. Since the big barn party at Luke's had been such a short time ago, Charity and Brandon—worn out from all the excitement—had wanted a small wedding. Just family and ranch hands. That suited her just fine.

She placed her hand on his forearm. "I can't believe Charity's all grown up. Seems like just yesterday you were walking her around the room, rocking her in your arms and begging her to go to sleep." She softly laughed. "The good ol' days."

He looked at her hand resting on his arm, but didn't respond.

"There's something I've been wanting to share with you, Flood, but seems the time was never quite right. I'd like to do that now."

He looked up with tortured, sad eyes. She remembered the first time she'd opened the cabin door, in a whiteout blizzard all those years ago, to the same amazing eyes that did wonderful things to her insides. She'd been fifteen, and him a few years older. Praise God, they'd been through a lot together. So many emotions moved across his face, she couldn't differentiate them all.

"Go on."

"I'll start with saying I love you." She couldn't stop her eyes from welling up. "I always have. And darn you for that too. That's why what I did when I was taken away to—"

He put a finger to her lips, silencing her voice but not the tears that crept over her lids to spill down her cheeks. A deep grief threatened to strangle her from the inside out. She hadn't wanted those other feelings for Luke's father. They'd just happened. And once they were there, they were a part of her, whether she liked it or not.

He wrapped an arm around her and pulled her close. "Shh, darlin'. You don't have to say a thing."

She pushed back, needing to see his face, his eyes. "I do, Flood," she said, wiping the tears off her cheeks with the sleeve of her wrapper. "Don't you see? This thing between us—my life in the Cheyenne village—will never go away unless I speak my mind. I don't want to hurt you. As God is my witness, he knows it. But I fear what will become of us if I don't."

Flood just stared at her with a stony expression. Was he as frightened as she?

"All right."

She swallowed, gathering her courage. "As the months passed and you didn't find me, my hope began to fade. The village moved several times. Rains washed away our tracks. Even the stars in the night sky looked different so many miles away from home. I changed—and yet, I was always the same. Anyway, I thought that perhaps, with the little boys to take care of at home, you'd stopped searching."

He picked up her hand and kissed it, his words fierce. "That would never happen."

"You understand what I'm trying not to say because it's just too painful?"

He nodded.

"About my Indian husband? Luke's father?" Oh, how she hated this, and yet, she loved it too. After all these years—to say it aloud was freeing. Now that he knew, whatever happened, they could get through it. She believed that with all her heart.

"Yes. You fell in love with him."

It sounded so odd coming from his lips. It was her turn to nod. "But I never stopped dreaming of coming home to you—and my little boys."

Suddenly her mind tumbled back to the Cheyenne village. She was fighting her way through the screaming, pain-inflicted gauntlet. Her nails ripped to the quick and chunks of her hair pulled out. Time and time again, sharp pain buffeted her head, but she pushed forward, pushed on, always refusing to fall. Flood's soul, deep in his eyes, appeared as battered and damaged as she'd felt then. She could hardly bear to look at him.

"But there's more, Flood. I finally told Luke everything. I hope you understand that I had to. He'd been carrying around so much guilt over what happened to me, and what I might have suffered at the hands of his father, that it wasn't right to keep the truth from him any longer. Telling him is one thing I don't regret at all, and I wish I'd done it sooner. He's been a different man ever since."

Flood swiped his hand across his face, then tipped his chin up and gazed at the beams of the ceiling. She saw him swallow as he blinked in quick succession. "I wondered about that." His raspy voice sent a shiver down her spine. "It was that morning about three years ago, when he came into breakfast dressed in his buckskins. You're right, he was a changed man. All for the better."

A bittersweet feeling gripped her. "Yes." She dared to reach out and place her hand on Flood's forearm, just below the roll of his sleeve. It was rough, warm. She closed her eyes for a moment, taking notice of all the sensations their connection created. She wasn't sure how he'd respond to all this—*to her*—after the truth was completely out in the open. At this moment, their steady, rock-hard relationship was anything but.

"And I'm so sorry if it hurts you to know that he knows. I am, Flood. I guess, life is hard, that's all. We do what we have to, to get through. Luke thinks of you as his father. He's told me that many times. He loves and respects you so much. All the boys do."

Flood turned and wrapped her in his arms. It was then that she knew everything would be all right. "That's good to hear, darlin'," he murmured, then softly kissed her lips. "It's hard for a flesh-and-blood man to live up to a dream. Luke has said the same to me. Now I just have to find a way to trust his words."

She wanted to pull him down to the bed, as was her habit, to make love, to share with each other all that God had given them, but she wasn't that sure of her standing just yet.

"You had nothing to do with your abduction," he went on. "It wasn't your fault." His voice was gritty and soft at the same time. "Nor were any of the feelings that grew as a result. I mean that, Claire. You're a survivor. You're even tougher than any of us realize. That's what's made our family so remarkable. I just wish I'd been able to find you quicker and bring you home. That's my only regret in all this." He kissed her hair, and she ran her hand up his chest. "Now, are you finished? Can we leave it at that?"

She nodded. "Yes." When she glanced up, she found tears on his face. It was almost her undoing.

"You sure?"

She nodded again, so thankful for the wonderful man she'd married and for the feel of his arms around her. Strong and safe—always her man. There was no one on this earth who could hold a candle to him, or to what he meant to her. She loved him now, in this moment, more than she ever had.

Chapter Thirty-Seven

Francis drew the buggy to a halt in front of the hotel. Brandon felt a little silly sitting in the back when he'd rather be driving, but Luke had insisted that Charity would be disappointed if they didn't arrive in style. A few streamers had been attached to the bumper, making him feel even sillier. Jack Jones stood out in front of the sheriff's office, smoking a cigarette as he watched the buggy with interest. Brandon gave Charity a quick peck on the lips. "We're here."

When she didn't respond, he looked at her questioningly, until he realized she was actually nervous. Could that be? Her strength and her confidence were two of the things he loved most about her. She could give as good as she got. He respected that. A feminine hothouse flower wouldn't fit into his world—nor would he want one.

He held back a chuckle. Well, she'd learn soon enough there wasn't anything to be nervous about. Tonight, he'd make sure she felt like a woman—*his woman*. He was up for the challenge.

Francis hopped out and grabbed their two small bags and carried them into the hotel. Earlier, he'd been griping that he was becoming a regular chauffeur, what with driving Hayden and Heather's wedding coach just last month. It was sort of a mean thing to ask him to do it again today—for Charity, considering his longtime crush on her. Oh well. What doesn't kill you makes you stronger.

Already outside the buggy, Brandon held out his hand to Charity, who still wore her mother's pretty white wedding dress.

"That sure fits you nice," he said, admiring her feminine attributes. The ones that were usually hidden away behind a chambray shirt and leather chaps. She placed her hand in his, and he pulled gently until she was settled on the boardwalk. Well aware they'd drawn more attention, he wrapped her in his arms and dipped her for a long kiss. She came up sputtering when clapping broke out from several different directions.

"Brandon! What's gotten into you? I thought you didn't like attracting attention to yourself."

"Seems you don't know everything about me, wife." Charity was finally his, and he could hardly believe it.

She cuffed him on the shoulder. "Well, watch it."

He took her hand and settled it in the crook of his elbow, then pushed open the door to Cattlemen's.

"I plan to, darlin'. Now, act like a lady. We're not on the ranch anymore."

She rolled her eyes. "You're incorrigible."

He laughed.

As they entered the lobby, Francis came back down the tall staircase, now empty-handed. He passed Brandon the key to their room.

"Bags are all inside," he said a bit sullenly. "Congratulations."

Charity smiled. "Thank you, Francis. Be ready. When you least expect it, you'll look into your own true love's eyes and fall hard."

His cheeks flushed red, but this time he didn't duck his head as he usually did.

"I don't know about that, Charity," he said. "I best be getting back to the ranch."

They watched Francis go until he disappeared out the door. The lobby was quiet. Still holding her hand, Brandon brought it to his mouth and kissed it, his gaze finding hers. "You ready to go up to our room, Mrs. Crawford? Or would you rather get another bite of dessert in the dining room? I'm game for whatever you'd like." If she was nervous, he didn't want to rush her.

She dropped her gaze. "No, I'm ready to go upstairs, Brandon." Her tone said different.

"That's my girl," he said teasingly, as he'd done for so many years.

Could this finally be happening? He felt as if he were walking on clouds as they ascended the staircase. How could he have ever thought going to Kansas City could replace this, their home? Y Knot, Montana, was nothing less than heaven on earth.

When Brandon opened the door to the only room on the top floor of Cattlemen's Hotel, Charity sucked in her breath. She'd never taken the time to look at the bridal suite, although she'd heard stories of it. Most people couldn't afford a room of such luxury, and stayed in their own homes after getting married. She noted several candles around the room, already lit, warming the walls in a golden glow. A pretty bouquet adorned a small table by the window, and another on the table beside the bed. She was glad now that she'd never taken the time to come up and see it. It made a wonderful memory that she'd hold dear for the rest of her life.

Brandon opened the top drawer of the dresser and extracted a small package. "For you."

"Oh, Brandon, you shouldn't have." With a shaky hand, she took the proffered gift.

"Go on and open it," he urged. "Kansas City didn't get all my money—though it tried."

Charity slipped the pink bow from around the small square box. Opening the lid, she found a beautiful heart-shaped silver locket dangling on a delicate chain.

"I thought when we got tired of the sights in Y Knot, we'd take a proper honeymoon somewhere special and have our pictures made. So you could put them inside. I know it's not much, but—"

She took his face between her palms. "It's the most beautiful necklace I've ever seen in my whole life. Thank you, my love."

Before she even had a chance to kiss and thank him correctly, he took her hand and led her across the room to the tall screen sectioning off a corner of the area. There, she found a bathtub already filled to the top with hot water. A big, fluffy towel sat folded and ready to be used, as did a dollop of soap. Charity went over, picked it up, and held it to her nose. "Roses."

"Yes. Just for you." It was as if he were looking into her soul. "When I was in Kansas City, this was all I could think about. This night and how I'd make it special for you."

"Oh, Brandon." She closed the distance between them and he wrapped her into his arms. The kiss was long, different from any she'd ever felt. They were man and wife. It was like no other feeling in the world.

"Turn around."

She did. He slowly undid the thirty-five buttons that ran down the back of her dress. He slipped one shoulder off and kissed her skin. Instantly, her breathing increased, and she tipped her head back, enjoying the way his lips made her skin tingle.

He gave a little nudge. "Go on now." He gestured to the tub. "Unless you want some company."

When her eyes went wide, he smiled and slowly backed away, pulling the screen over so she'd have complete privacy.

"Take your time. It's not often you get to soak in a big tub on the top floor of Cattlemen's. I'll just be out here, wondering what you're up to. If you need me to scrub your back, just holler."

The first sunbeam that danced through the window woke Charity. She stretched, then reached out her leg until her foot touched something warm. Instinctively, she pulled it back, surprised. Then her wonderful memories of last night came racing back, putting a smile on her lips. She rolled over until she was close to Brandon, watching him sleep.

Oh, how she loved him. She'd thought she loved him before, but that paled in light of being married and everything that meant. Unable to stop herself, she reached out and touched his lips.

He opened his eyes. "Morning, sunshine."

She giggled. "It's sunshine now, is it?"

"You bet. How'd you sleep?"

Enough of small talk. She'd learned plenty last night to know she liked being married. And that her husband was the most handsome, desirable man in the whole world. How she'd gotten him, she'd never know. Just thinking about her wedding night made her mind go all squiggly inside. She didn't want to waste another moment chatting when there were other better, more fascinating things to do.

Brandon chuckled. "I take it your silence means you *slept* really darn good."

She scooted closer. "You're right." She didn't want to appear eager, but dang, she couldn't help it. She leaned in and gave him a quick kiss on the lips. "Really, *really* good—and more." She smiled into his face.

Wrapping her in his arms, Brandon rolled her over, kissing her until she thought she might faint. His fingers combed through her hair, then moved down to her shoulders. A puff of air floated in through the open window, cooling her heated skin. She slid her hand over his bare chest, loving the feel of his skin beneath her palm.

Just then, a knock sounded on the door. Brandon looked over. "Already?" He picked up the small clock on the bedside table, then pulled the sheet up and covered her. "I didn't expect them for another hour. That's what I get for assuming."

Charity blinked, fascinated with the view of his strong, bare arm. "Who?"

"Breakfast, my darling." He quickly kissed her lips, then drew back, and his crafty smile made her giggle.

Another knock, this one a bit louder. "Good morning, *Mr. and Mrs.* Crawford. Your breakfast has arrived."

It was Lenore Saffelberg. Suddenly, the melodic strumming of a mandolin wafted in through the open bedroom window.

"Would it be rude of me to ask her to go away?" Brandon asked. It was clear he had other things on his mind.

Charity laughed softly. "Yes—and be quiet! She might hear you."

"I have an idea. Let's send her away and eat later in the restaurant."

"We'll be right there," Charity called, loving the desire she saw in her husband's eyes.

"Taaaake your time. I have nothing better to do than stand out here in the hall, smelling your coffee and flapjacks."

Charity pushed Brandon out of the bed. "Hurry up! You know how snippy she can get." Charity bolted up too, and pulled on her white silk wrapper, enjoying the feel of its loving caress.

"On my way." Brandon finished buttoning his shirt, then pulled open the door.

Behind him, Charity gasped. There stood Roady, holding their breakfast tray, a pretty yellow daisy clenched between his teeth. Lenore, Luke, Matt, and Mark surrounded him. Francis and Lucky crowded in, all with big grins on their faces.

Roady plucked the flower from his teeth and dropped it back in the white porcelain bud vase on the tray.

"*Goooood* mornin', you two," he drawled. "We didn't want you to feel lonely or anything on your first morning as man and wife. So we all decided to come over and keep you company."

Charity's heart swelled. So many people she loved—and who loved her right back. She was blessed mightily—especially with her magnificent new husband, who turned to look at her with a crooked smile on his face.

"The wives wouldn't come," Luke said, over Roady's head. "Said visiting this soon was in poor taste. But we didn't think so, did we, boys?" Everyone shook their heads in mock innocence.

"No siree," Matt said, then chuckled. "Not after all the years of torment our dear little sister has put us through. It's payback time for all the temper tantrums, hoodwinking, manipulation—"

"Hey," Charity protested. She crossed her arms over her chest, feeling a mite conspicuous—but happy too.

Luke nudged Roady forward. "Get on in there, Roady. We have some celebrating to do."

About the Author

Caroline Fyffe was born in Waco, Texas, the first of many towns she would call home during her father's career with the US Air Force. A horse aficionado from an early age, she earned a Bachelor of Arts in communications from California State University-Chico before launching what would become a twenty-year career as an equine photographer. She began writing fiction to pass the time during long days in the show arena, channeling her love of horses and the Old West into a series of Western historicals. Her debut novel, *Where the Wind Blows*, won the Romance Writers of America's prestigious Golden Heart Award as well as the Wisconsin RWA's Write Touch Readers' Award. She and her husband have two grown sons and live in the Pacific Northwest.

Sign up for Caroline's newsletter: www.carolinefyffe.com
See her Equine Photography: www.carolinefyffephoto.com
LIKE her FaceBook Author Page:
Facebook.com/CarolineFyffe
Twitter: @carolinefyffe
Write to her at: caroline@carolinefyffe.com

Printed in Great Britain
by Amazon